COMMUNICATION

THROUGH THE AGES

— An Indian Perspective —

COMMUNICATION
THROUGH THE AGES
— An Indian Perspective —

Edited by

Lakhan Mehrotra
Raghavendra Vajpeyi

ARYAN BOOKS INTERNATIONAL
New Delhi
in association with
MEDIA INDIA CENTRE FOR RESEARCH
AND DEVELOPMENT
Gurgaon

COMMUNICATION THROUGH THE AGES:
AN INDIAN PERSPECTIVE

ISBN: 978-81-7305-373-3

Published in **2009** by:

ARYAN BOOKS INTERNATIONAL
Pooja Apartments, 4B, Ansari Road, New Delhi - 110 002 (India)
Tel.: 23287589, 23255799; Fax: 91-11-23270385
E-mail: aryanbooks@vsnl.com, aryanbooks@gmail.com

in association with

MEDIA INDIA CENTRE FOR RESEARCH AND DEVELOPMENT
Gurgaon

Computer Typeset and Printed in India at
ABI Prints & Publishing Co., New Delhi

Dedicated to the spirit of journalists and
communicators who did not agree
to abdicate their professional
commitment and succumb
to any pressure of those
in power and
authority.

Foreword

It gives me pleasure in writing a 'Foreword' for the *Communication through the Ages: An Indian Perspective* edited by Lakhan Mehrotra and Raghavendra Vajpeyi. The book is 'dedicated to the spirit of journalists and communicators who did not agree to abdicate their professional commitment and succumb to any pressure of those in power and authority'. Late Upendra Vajpeyi was a perfect example of such a journalist. From my personal knowledge I know that the dedication is essentially in memory of Upendra Vajpeyi who possessed these qualities in ample measures. The dedication is much more pertinent since this book had been planned by him and he had collected these articles on its impressive themes in his lifetime itself. My pleasure is much more since I knew him personally, though rather late, only when I came in contact with his plans to establish the National Media Centre. The NMC is a testimony to Upendra Vajpeyi's commitment, zeal and sincerity that was phenomenal.

Communication means transformation of information, thoughts and messages. The means of communication have been continuously changing through the ages. The basic forms in the beginning were signs and through speech. A basic change in evolution came, that was fundamental, when writing came into existence. Book publishing and journalism facilitated the wide spread dissemination and preservation of information. Mass media, for over a century, has played a major role in changing the social, economic and educational institutions. Recent advances in electronics have brought out major changes in communication. Cellular telephony has made personal communication inexpensive and widespread. Worldwide computer networks allow computer users to use modems to communicate rapidly.

The book is divided into two sections. Section I deals with the concept, purpose, nature and tools of communication. A.S. Bais, Shilpi Narang have contributed on medical aspects and strategies needed for impaired people. Lakhan Mehrotra philosophically deals with the nature of connectivity of man with his mentor (the God), an all pervasive force that governs the universe. Archaeologist S.P. Gupta has described how the Upper Palaeolithic man, over 18,000 years ago, had ably communicated his views on economy, society and religion etc. Photojournalism happens to be one of the most difficult and risky assignments of a journalist. Manish Swarup has shown how the American public opinion went against the military offensive showing the sufferings of Vietnamese people. Swarup's experience of three theatres of war in Afghanistan, Iraq and Kargil is worth going through. S.P. Dikshit describes the Urdu newspaper, *Nazm,* that happens to be the first one entirely produced in poetry. I wonder if there are many such examples. Ramamohan Rao's rich experience in responsible government assignments is reflected in his article on the scope of information and communication policy of successive governments in India. Raghavendra Vajpeyi has traced the history of communication in India through the ages.

Section II deals with visual manifestations of means of communication as living organisms are capable of presenting themselves through the medium of performing arts, which, in my personal view, is a very important medium. Nishi Misra's article on folk songs, Kavita Nagpal's exposition of theatre's capability in establishing direct communication between the artist and the audience are very lucid expositions of that medium of communication. K.P. Srivastava connects the world of music and dance in his 'emotions recollected in tranquility'. Shovana Narayan has effectively demonstrated the ability of Kathak dance as a medium of communication. Raja-Radha Reddy has exposed the traditional relationship of Kuchipudi dance style with the tenets of the *Bharatanatyasastra.* Sucharita Khanna has very ably established the relationship among cosmology-cum-mythology, classical Sanskrit literature, aesthetics and Bharata Natyam dance.

I have found the book very interesting and worth reading. And as a scientist and educationist, I have enjoyed going through its manuscript very thoroughly.

P.N. Srivastava

Preface

The present book entitled, *Communication through the Ages: An Indian Perspective,* defines communication in its most expandable sense as man's desire and effort to connect himself with others at all levels of his experience, knowledge and consciousness – occasionally out stepping the mundane level to enter the supra mundane level. Thought processes have been considered as the valid manifestation of the inner working of unconscious mind – the real powerhouse and its counterpart the conscious mind being just the operating switch-board. Inclusion of articles on different themes on the basis of their well considered parameters has the logic of acceptance of conventional as well as non-conventional methods for enquiry. This makes the work a novel experiment and experience. All this happens to be a fair enough justification for this study.

Two methods of enquiry have been followed by different scholars, viz., archaeological method and religio-philosophical method. While archaeological method adheres to the principle of known to less known to unknown, but the other method reposes its faith in receipt of signals, followed by message and experience leading to knowledge and enlightenment. Although the former allows the possibility of laboratory test, examination and assessment of facts and their evaluation in a scientific manner, the latter has faith in concentration, feeling and experience as the method which precedes the receipt of knowledge leading to enlightenment. The logic in the latter case happens to be: what we know is far less than what we do not know, and what we do not know does not necessarily mean that it does not exist at all. That may be because of the absence in our knowledge of methods and means and tools of knowing it.

Man's innate desire to connect himself with his creator, happens to be the theme of philosophical enquiry. It is followed by another article contributed by a famous astrologer who claims that heavenly bodies and planetary configuration happen to be the extra-terrestrial signs and signals which foretell about the things to take place. The Upanishadic method, of question-answer has been applied in the third article in the series in its attempt to understand how two different ideologies – Brahmanical and Jain ideologies agree to tackle the issues of worldly existence, death, death related rituals and rebirth or reincarnation in their *Bhagavadgita* context. In such cases, we tend to accept inadequacy of our understanding of the method as well as superiority of the knowledge of the learned scholars.

Growth of science and technology has been a major contributor to expansion of education and information programming in its print and electronic media context. Satellite television and Edusat have been found major players in the spread of information, knowledge and education to their farthest level.

Theatre, folk music, classical music as well as regional classical dance styles like Kathak, Kuchipudi and Bharata Natyam have been included among constantly developing audiovisual means of communication which keep on making sincere efforts to relate themselves to societal and situational realities, instead of confining themselves to their stereotype models of the past.

We hope that this study will be of some interest to the lay readers and specialists alike.

(R.V.)

Contents

SECTION II

Print Media, Visual and Performing Arts

Acknowledgements

We thank the following contributors (mentioned in alphabetical order) for their valuable articles published in this volume:

Professors A.S. Bais, and S.P. Dikshit, Dr. S.P. Gupta, Ms. Shanti Hiranand, Dr. Sucharita Khanna, Mr. Lakhan Mehrotra, Ms. Nishi Misra, Drs. Rajendra Mishra and Sunil Misra, Ms. Kavita Nagpal, Dr. Shilpi Narang, Ms. Shovana Narayan, Professor K.N. Rao, Mr. I. Ramamohan Rao, Dr. Raja Radha Reddy, Ms. Malavika Sarukkai, Mr. K.P. Srivastava, Mr. Manish Swarup, Dr. Raghavendra Vajpeyi and Mr. Upendra Vajpeyi.

Unfortunately our two contributors, viz., Dr. Gupta and Mr. Vajpeyi are no more with us.

Dr. Reddy deserves special thanks for allowing us to consult his personal copy of the *Bharata Natyasastra*.

Mr. Lakhan Mehrotra, an erudite scholar and a senior Indian diplomat, had very kindly accepted Mr. Vajpeyi's request to go through the manuscript of the book and to assess intrinsic value of articles included in it. We are thankful to him for spending some quality time on going through the articles and making valuable remarks and suggestions.

Ms. Aruna Patel and Mr. O.P. Tandon deserve credit for allowing me freehand in preparation of the manuscript.

We thank Mr. Tandon for convincing M/s Aryan Books International to become joint publisher of this book.

Mr. V. Gopinathan deserves our thanks for undertaking the task of preparation and computer printing of the manuscript.

We also thank Mr. Vikas Arya of M/s Aryan Books International for bringing out the *Communication through the Ages: An Indian Perspective* well in time.

(R.V.)

Roman Equivalents of Nāgarī Letters

अ	a	आ	ā	इ	i	ई	ī	उ	u	ऊ	ū
ए	e	ऐ	ai	ओ	o	औ	au	ऋ	ṛi		
क्	k	ख्	kh	ग्	g	घ्	gh	ङ्	ṅ		
च्	ch	छ्	chh	ज्	j	झ्	jh	ञ्	ñ		
ट्	t	ठ्	th	ड्	d	ढ्	dh	ण्	ṇ		
त्	t	थ्	th	द्	d	ध्	dh	न्	n		
प्	p	फ्	ph	ब्	b	भ्	bh	म्	m		
य्	y	र्	ṛ	ल	l	व्	v				
श्	ś	ष	sh	स्	s	ह्	h				
क्ष्	ksh	त्र्	tr	ज्ञ्	jñ						

अनुस्वार Anusvāra ṁ

विसर्ग : Visarga ḥ

List of Contributors

Prof. P.N. Srivastava
Chancellor, Manipur Central University, Imphal & Chairman, National Board of Accreditation, AICTE; Former Vice-Chancellor, JNU, New Delhi & Member, Planning Commission, Government of India, New Delhi.

Prof. A.S. Bais
Former Head of ENT Department and Principal of Lady Hardinge Medical College.

Dr. Shilpi Narang
Specialist in Hearing Aids, Director, Alps.

Mr. Lakhan Mehrotra
Former Secretary, Ministry of External Affairs, Government of India, UN Secretary General's Special Representative in Cambodia and UN envoy in Indonesia.

Prof. K.N. Rao
Retired Auditor General of India, a well known Astrologer and Editor of Astrological Magazine.

Acharya Mahapragya
Revered Jain Muni.

Dr. S.P. Gupta
A renowned archaeologist, art historian and Chairman, Indian Archaeological Society and former Director, Allahabad Museum.

Dr. Raghavendra Vajpeyi
Department of History, Delhi University.

Dr. Rajendra Mishra
Director, Consortium of Educational Communication.

Dr. Sunil Misra
Director, Audience Research, All India Radio, Prof. & Head of Department of Survey of Programme Evaluation, IGNOU.

Mr. Manish Swarup
News Photographer, Associated Press and NFI & PII Awardee for photography.

Mr. I. Ramamohan Rao
Former Principal Information Officer, Govt. of India and Media Adviser to Defence Minister, GOI and has been a Media Adviser to the state of Punjab, J&K and Haryana.

Prof. Surya Prasad Dikshit
Former Head of the Department of Hindi and Modern India Languages and Department of Journalism, Lucknow University.

Ms. Nishi Misra
Hindi Department, Gyan Bharati School.

Ms. Kavita Nagpal
Theatre Personality and Drama Critic.

Mr. K.P. Srivastava
Senior Journalist and disciple of Kathak Guru Kishen Maharaj.

Ms. Shanti Hiranand
Eminent Exponent of Indian Classical Music (Hindustani). She has been nationally awarded for her accomplishment.

Dr. Sucharita Khanna
A teacher and performer of the Bharatanatyam style of Dance, Post-graduate degree from Baroda University and PhD. from BHU, Varanasi. Presently she is Director of Kalanidhi, a Centre of Performing Arts and author of *Dancing Divinities in Indian Art*.

Ms. Malavika Sarukkai
Internationally known exponent of Bharata Natyam Dance from Karnataka.

Dr. Raja Radha Reddy
Popular Kuchipudi Dancers, imparting training in the same discipline; recipients of national and international honours.

Ms. Shovana Narayan
A very versatile and eminent exponent of Kathak Dance. She has been conferred with a number of national and international awards for excellence in dance.

Introduction

Mr. Upendra Vajpeyi enjoyed a reasonably long standing of a thoroughly professional journalist who had the advantage of personally knowing many political leaders of the country. He fondly recalled several occasions of his exchange of views with them on issues of national and international significance. Although he happened to know many people, their personal views and reservations about things and people and their public gestures on them, he never betrayed them on any occasion. So also, he never revealed his source of information without its formal authorization. That is, he sincerely believed in keeping all channels of communication open and active, by remaining a responsible member of journalist community.

He also had the privilege of participating in many conferences, seminars and symposia in India as well as in other countries. Not only that, he himself organized several conferences, etc. in the capacity of the founder-general secretary of the National Media Centre (New Delhi). Further, his relatively long association and communication with cross-section of the Indian society convinced him about necessity and relevance of some India centric book on communication which could evoke interest of lay reader and could also serve academic needs of students pursuing some course in journalism and communication.

Once Mr. Vajpeyi had that clarity of perspective, he pursued his dream in the right earnest. He contacted several knowledgeable people who could put across their views in simple and lucid language and who belonged to diverse disciplines – ranging from medical sciences to music, theology and philosophy to pre-history and history, print and electronic media to photo-journalism; and also from folk music to Hindustani classical music; and from theatre to regional dance styles, (i.e., Bharata Natyam, Kuchipudi and Kathak dance styles) – their theoretical bases, as well as their relevance as living systems of communication capable of adjusting themselves according to needs of changing time. He (Mr. Vajpeyi) was immensely successful in availing consent of some eminent personalities and also their articles on themes and areas of their own choice.

All this happened towards the fag end of the life of the National Media Centre, which after accomplishing its aims and objectives, arrived at unanimous decision to dissolve itself on September 01, 2007. And the present Media India Centre for Research & Development came into existence as its successor institution. It took upon itself the responsibility of fulfilling the commitment of the former about publication of volume on communication.

Unfortunately, Mr. Vajpeyi fell critically ill and passed away on 17th February 2008. The *MIC/R&D* has taken the decision to fulfil his last wish by publishing the book, i.e. *Communication through the Ages: An Indian Perspective,* in the manner and spirit he had envisaged it.

This collection comprises of twenty academic contributions, classified into two sections reflecting two separate strands of thought:

Section I has a strong theoretical bias in favour of idea, concept, purpose, nature and scope, and means and tools of communication. This section has twelve articles. Professor A.S. Bais has in his article discussed the structure of ear and its significance in communication. Dr. Shilpi Narang has, likewise, focused her attention on problems of hearing impaired people and strategies needed for improving their lot. Next three articles have been devoted to the examination of unusual and untraditional methods of communication (virtually entering the fields of theology, philosophy and the mysteries the world beyond our normal sensory perception). Mr. Lakhan Mehrotra has, in his article on 'communication with the unseen', examined the nature of connectivity of man with his mentor (the God) through the means of understanding and realization. Professor K.N. Rao has in his article indicated the role of extra terrestrial communication in the form of different planetary positions and their equally different influences on nature and man alike. The third article in this series reproduces Mr. Upendra Vajpeyi's dialogue with Acharya Mahapragya on the underlying bases of the concept of incarnation, reincarnation and death and rituals related with it – and their rationale in the light of their exposition in the *Bhagavadgita*. The next two contributions return to the material world. Thus, Dr. S.P. Gupta has, in his learned paper, posited how the Upper Palaeolithic Man had ably communicated his views on economy, society, religion and magic to his contemporary people through thematically illustrated paintings on the inner walls of Rock Shelters in India and elsewhere (some 18000 years Before Present). Invention of writing as an alternative and effective means of communication took place some 12000 years later. Dr. Raghavendra Vajpeyi has documented in his article the story of communication in India from the earliest time down to the advent of the modern age. The next two articles underline the significance of satellite programming and television telecasts in the spread of information and communication. Thus, Dr. Rajendra Mishra has shown in his article how the satellite technology has successfully offered a real breakthrough in planning, programming and presentation of programmes made on education for the target audience of students and teachers alike – all because of the availability of the Edusat facility. Dr. Sunil Misra's article also adopts near identical approach to the problems of population awareness related strategies in their radio-television centric presentation. Mr. Manish Swarup has competently made out the case of justification for photo-journalism as one of the most potent means of communication. He has shown in his article how the American public opinion had gone against the American military offensive in the Vietnam war – because of publication and telecast of photographs showing suffering of the Vietnamese people. Mr. Swarup's experience of three theatres of war, viz., Afghanistan, Iraq and Kargil, underlines the fact that photo-journalism happens to be one of the most difficult and risky assignments of a journalist; but also that it becomes equally rewarding and commendable when he receives applause and acclaim for coverage of the conflict zone. Mr. Ramamohan Rao's contribution sheds welcome light on purpose, nature and scope of information and communication policy of succeeding governments in India-right from the time of Hickey's *Gazette* down to the present day. It rightly makes plea for change of mindset of bureaucracy on right to information. Professor S.P. Dikshit has, in his well researched and ably presented article (in Hindi), underlined the fact that the late 19th century Urdu newspaper, *Nazm*, published from Lucknow, happened to be the first newspaper of its kind. It was entirely produced in poetry, a unique concept in the tradition of newspaper publication and that such a style had not been tried till then either in India or anywhere in the world.

Section II deals with visual manifestations of means of communication as living organisms capable of presenting themselves through the medium of performing arts. It has another set of eight articles in it. Ms. Nishi Misra has made in her article a strong plea in favour of folk songs as an effective means of communication. Ms. Kavita Nagpal's article examines theatre's capability in establishing direct communication link between the theatre people and their target audience – virtually both having an equal sense of participation in the action taking place there. Mr. K.P. Srivastava has relived his long association with celebrities of the world of music and dance in his 'emotions recollected in tranquility' piece. Ms. Shanti Hiranand, herself a renowned musician, has in her article shown that music happens to be an effective means of communication. Dr. Sucharita Khanna's article tries to establish relationship among cosmology-cum-mythology, classical Sanskrit literature, plastic art, aesthetics and Bharata Natyam dance style. Ms. Malavika Sarukkai has discussed the nature and scope of Bharata Natyam as the dance style which happens to be a living discipline capable of undergoing time honoured developments and changes. She loves to call it 'speaking in the present tense'. Dr. Raja Radha Reddy has been eminently successful in showing the traditional relationship of the Kuchipudi dance style with the tenets of the *Bharata Natyasastra.* He has suggested that, despite its classical base, Kuchipudi dance style continues to remain in harmony with the changing times – all because of its capacity to develop, change and adjust with situational demands. Ms. Shovana Narayan's article on 'Kathak dance as an effective medium of communication' happens to be a well researched piece on the Kathak tradition and dance style. It clearly establishes that the Kathak dance style had existed as early as in the fourth century BC and that it happened to be different from that of the kathaka-bards who sang songs in praise of rulers on the occasions of religious ceremonies, etc. as well as in royal courts and public places. Ms. Narayan has also quoted evidence of a Prakrit Text (which flourished in the fourth century BC) and which has mentioned Kathak dance as a respectable form of entertainment. According to that Text, one such recital had taken place in the court of the ruler of Varanasi, King Adinatha. That is, performance of Kathak dance recital in elite gatherings and in royal courts had been a time honoured tradition.

I have taken cue from Mr. Mehrotra's observations and remarks on the first draft of articles regarding editing of the book. I have tried to correct and standardize spellings, as well as to Romanize equivalents of Sanskrit words and strokes occurring in the articles. So also, I have meticulously tried to cross-check and put references in footnotes.

Likewise, I have taken the liberty of inserting footnotes, here and there in the articles, by way of observations and remarks as pieces of additional evidence, either in support of argument in the main text or to show that some evidence exists which does not agree with the opinion/remark of the author.

I also accept responsibility for the errors and mistakes which may still be present in the book.

(R.V.)

SECTION I

Idea, Concept, Nature, Scope and Means of Communication

1

Human Communications

A.S. Bais

The special sense organs which we possess are nose, tongue and ears. Our extraordinary ability to hear, smell and taste allows us to connect with the rest of the world. To understand its mechanism we must know a bit of its anatomy and functioning first.

ANATOMY OF THE EAR

Anatomically the ear is divided into three parts:

a. External ear which consists of Pinna, Ear Drum and the External ear canal
b. Middle ear with its Eustachian tube and small ossicles, namely Malleus, Incus and Stapes are known as middle ear cleft
c. Inner ear also known as Labyrinth comprises of cochlea, vestibule and semicircular canals.

A and B are concerned with conduction of sound while C for perception of sound.

The ear subserves the function of not only the hearing but also maintains the body equilibrium while the cochlea, 8th cranial nerve and the cortical centres are concerned with reception, processing and transmission of sound. The vestibular part of the Labyrinth along with the semicircular canal are concerned with maintenance of balance of the body. The impulses come from the eyes, joints, tactile, muscular and visceral senses. The information regarding position of the head is provided by the Labyrinth so that one can adjust his body accordingly.

The inner ear is the only human organ of the body which develops full adult size very early in the intra uterine life. The baby in the womb hears the sound perfectly well and if the sound is loud and not to its liking then it changes its position, besides his heart beat also goes up. The story of Abhimanyu in the epic *Mahābhārata* is not imaginative but true.

Larynx (the voice box) is the most beautiful organ of human body. The outline of the Larynx is readily seen in lean males. It is located slightly higher in the neck of neonates and women. Its position is on the contrary lower in the aged.

During swallowing and phonation the external muscles of the larynx move it up and down. The mobility of the larynx is a functional necessity. The larynx moves because its muscles are connected through the agency of the hyoid bone with the tongue and the Jaw bone superiorly and the sternum and the collar bone (clavicle) inferiorly.

It has also a framework of cartilage. During inspiration the lumen of the larynx gets dilated. There are also three muscles which narrows the lumen of the larynx to perform the vocal function. The vocal cords are two in number and during speech production vibrate because of its tensile-strength and elasticity and approximate with each other. Failure to approximate will alter the quality of voice.

The nose is the central part of the face and a very versatile organ of the human body and can be poked in to places where it does not belong. Besides, it adds to one's beauty and charm. As it is the most prominent part of the face people like to give blows on it during fights. Further, it is crushed or deformed in road accidents and in the past was cut as a part of punishment especially when someone's character was suspected.

The main functions of the nose are as follows:

1. Respiratory Channel
2. Olfaction (smell)
3. Protective function consisting of warming the inhaled air, its moistening & filtering.

About 40 to 60 per cent of dust particles and bacteria inspired with the air are retained in the nose and then removed from it with the mucus. This function is performed with the special lining of nose which has cilias.

The sneezing and watering from the eyes are also important protective mechanisms.

4. The resonating function of the nose accounts for the special timbre of the human voice.

The sense of smell and taste determine the flavour of food and also warn us of environmental pollution such as gas leakage, air pollution and spoiled food. Olfactory dysfunction could be due to nasal and sinus disorders, brain disease or Alzheimer's disease. The receptors for olfaction are situated high in the nasal vault.

Dysfunction of smell can be classified as Anosmia which means loss of smell function. Parosmia means perversion of sense of smell, a good odour may smell as a bad odour. Hyperosmia means increased sensibility which is seen in neurotic individuals.

Sensation such as sweet, sour, bitter, salty and metallic are mediated via taste buds. The receptors are located over the dorsal surface of the tongue, margin of the tongue, soft palate and pharynx.

The ability to hear the sounds and understand its meaning occurs very quickly in life. This helps us in learning a new language. It is acquired quickly by a child than by an adult. We have the extraordinary ability to master the language and use it to our advantage. The animals have to sniff or smell and have to listen to their enemies' sounds to protect themselves.

A child acquires speech by hearing. In fact, the tendency to imitate is inborn. If a child has no island of hearing he will never acquire speech and will suffer from speech and hearing disability. Fortunately some island of hearing is always there in majority of the deaf cases, which can be beneficial if the diagnosis of hearing disability is made very early in life. If the baby does not respond to mother's gesture language and if she starts suspecting that her child does not hear then the treating doctor should take prompt action in its proper management. The saying goes right "catch them young". Everyone can be wrong but a mother cannot be wrong. If she thinks of hearing disability then it should not be passed off as a case of delayed milestone. Proper rehabilitative steps if taken promptly can help him/her to become a useful member of the society.

Animals have the remarkable ability to move their pinna to collect the sound source so that any danger perceived is passed on very quickly to its fellow animals. Human beings cannot rotate their pinnas as they are attached to the side of the skull by two to three poorly developed muscles. However we can always push it forward by the flat of the palm to bring them near the sound source to collect the sound and hear. This phenomenon is more noticeable in elderly who do it to improve their hearing ability.

In order to survive in this world we need to communicate either verbally or by using gesture language. Our special sense organs play a very important role in this activity. We nod our head when we agree, we move it to and fro when we do not agree. When we do not know or are surprised then we shrug our shoulders. If we shrivel our nose then we have indicated that the particular smell is not to our liking. If one touches someone's hand or any sensitive part of the body then one has communicated his desire. Probably its our sixth sense or the telepathy which works.

Animals always produce sounds to declare their presence. The predators get a warning by these sounds. Sometimes they also attract a female by producing a different kind of a sound and also succeed in conveying their desire to mate. Elephants have the ability to hear sound up to 4 km and this helps them to keep contact with their families if one has gone deep into the forest or elsewhere. Some animals urinate excessively on a tree to demarcate their territory or by their droppings convey their desire to mate as it provides information regarding the reproductive condition of the female (Glatston, 1979). Smell of urine warns other animals to keep off their territory as it acts as a check post. What a wonderful way of communication.

Human beings, by using their special sense organs, communicate emotions to others. During stress we sweat excessively, or change our expressions on the face. The chemistry of love can be triggered between male and female by one's emotional behaviour for which not much of talking is required.

Positive or negative emotions can be passed on from person to person very quickly. A sensitive person is more prone to catch the mood of others. Intellectual and emotional modes of communication can be passed from one to another in which these special sense organs play a very significant role.

BIBLIOGRAPHY

Colino, Stacey, *That look, it is catching*, The Washington Post.
Gopichand, T., *Otorhinolaryngology*, 1994.
Glatston, *Internet*, 1979.
Maqbool, Mohammad, *Text Book of Ear, Nose & Throat diseases*, 1982.
Palchun, V.T. and N.L. Voznesensky, *Diseases of the Ear - Throat & Nose*, Mir Publishers, Moscow, first edition, 1998.

2

Hearing Impairment – How Risky

Shilpi Narang

Long back Helen Keller had said:

> I donot want peace passeth understanding. I want the understanding which bringeth peace.
>
> The sentence is full of interpretations, in its own way, spelling out the basic tenets of communication.
>
> One view is that if you cannot hear, you cannot understand.

Evidently, the human body is an integrated whole. Each component of the body has its own identity, playing its specific role. Whatever the claims of individual components of the human apparatus, it is intended to be serving a higher purpose. The higher or sublime purpose in Helen Keller's concept should be understood as consolidating peace which is clue to sustenance of society.

In more concrete terms, one of the basic tenets of communication is 'if you cannot hear, you cannot understand'. There may be other channels of understanding in the human system. In fact, there are. But hearing had been playing the crucial role. Any indifference towards loss of hearing may lead to most disastrous consequences, not only individually but socially, politically and in many other ways. Any hearing loss or impairment, whether as a result of childhood disease or excessive noise pollution, results in not being fully part of our friends and families. Not understanding what people are saying may turn out to be the beginning of the end of communication.

At the same time, it is important to realize that hearing aids can improve communication by up to 90 per cent. But the stigma attached in seeking such help still keeps people away from this significant aid.

Some time back, a nine-year old child diagnosed with hearing loss came to my clinic. An academically bright child all along, he had been lagging behind in school. The reason was simple. He couldn't hear.

I suggested a hearing aid, but his parents were too embarrassed to admit their child had a problem. This kind of problem becomes acute in old age. Old people with a steady loss in hearing become prone to feeling excluded. The answer is simple: a hearing aid.

If Helen Keller were born today, her life would undoubtedly have been completely different. Her life long dream was to be able to talk, something that she was never really able to attain. Today, the technology exists which would have helped Helen and people like her, to communicate independently with the world.

Worldwide, 278 million people are estimated to have moderate to profound hearing loss in both ears.

80% of deaf and hearing-impaired people live in low-and middle-income countries.

The major preventable causes of hearing impairment in low- and middle-income countries are middle ear infections, excessive noise, inappropriate use of certain drugs, problems during childbirth and vaccine-preventable infections.

One quarter of cases of hearing impairment begin during childhood.

At least half of all hearing impairment is avoidable.

Immunization against childhood diseases such as measles, meningitis, rubella and mumps is key to preventing hearing impairment.

Properly fitted hearing aids can improve communication in at least 90% of people with hearing impairment.

In developing countries, fewer than 1 in 40 people who need a hearing aid have different types of hearing loss such as 'conductive deafness', 'Sensory Neural Deafness', 'Mixed Hearing Loss' and 'Central Hearing Loss'. The degree of hearing loss is termed as 'mild', 'moderate', 'moderately severe', 'severe' and 'profound'. Educationally hearing loss is termed on the basis of the stages in a child's development when the loss occurred: congenital – from birth, 'prelingual' before the acquisition of language by a child, 'post-lingual' – after the child has acquired language and 'post-vocational'.

The main causes of deafness are heredity, accident and illness. In about 80% of all cases of deafness, genetic factor/heredity, auto toxic drugs, rubella or other viral infections contracted by the pregnant mother are probable causes of deafness. Constant noise level can cause progressive and eventually severe sensory neural hearing loss. Similarly, tumours, exposure to explosive sound, injury to skull or ear could lead to deafness.

APPENDIX I: NUMBER ONE DISABILITY IN THE WORLD – HEARING LOSS

According to a study in September 2007, hearing loss had become the number one disability in the world with loud music, recreational equipment and noisy workplaces causing one-third of all such cases, according to a new study. The study, which came ahead of World Deafness Day on September 24, estimates that around 500 million people worldwide suffer from some form of hearing loss.

Another alarming information of the study is the people are now losing their hearing at a much younger age than they used to 30 years ago, the study compiled by the Hearing Institute of America said. The revelation has raised concern among experts in India, who feel such ailments are increasing rapidly. About 1-2 per 1,000 children across the world are born hearing impaired. In India, the figure is likely to be higher at about 3-4 children per 1,000. "Out of the total deaf population of 6.3 per cent in India, about one per cent suffers from noise induced deafness."

The youth in India are becoming more prone to hearing-related problems. "It is a real matter of concern, especially at a time when young students are hooked to their mobile phones and music players for long hours", according to ENT specialist R.C. Deka of the AIIMS, New Delhi.

APPENDIX II: BEWARE OF HANDS-FREE EARPHONES

The Indian youth is fast becoming hearing impaired, thanks to the increased use of electronic gadgets like the 'hands free' earphones.

Hearing impairment takes a heavy social and emotional toll. It is known to cause fatigue, tension, stress and depression; and leads to withdrawal from social situations, which cause rejection and loneliness. It reduces alertness and increases risk to personal safety, impairs memory and the ability to learn new task, reduces job performance and earning power and impacts negatively on overall health. As much as 20 per cent of hearing disability is caused at birth or immediately thereafter.

APPENDIX III: VOICE AS IDENTIFICATION

Your voice identifies you. A hoarse voice is the first complaint when there is a problem in the voice box. Roughness of voice results from variation of periodicity and intensity of consecutive sound waves. For production of normal voice the vocal cord should be able to approximate properly with each other, have a proper size and stiffness; and an ability to vibrate regularly in response to the air column.

Voice is an extremely sensitive indicator of emotional status and general health. Therefore when evaluating voice disorder, the entire physical and psychological status should be considered. Altered function in nearly any part of the body can result in vocal changes, according to Dr. Ravi K. Viswanathan, Director AVM Medical ENT Research Foundation, Chennai.

APPENDIX IV: RECOGNIZE INDIAN SIGN LANGUAGE

The hearing impaired people have demanded official recognition to Indian Sign Language (ISL).

The National Association of the Deaf has complained that deaf persons are constantly being stigmatized and discriminated against by the authorities and the public at large. There is a complete lack of awareness of ISL, as even teachers for the hearing-impaired do not know this language. Also, there is no provision for ISL interpreters in Government offices; hospitals, courts and other public places.

MARGINALIZATION

"This lack of effective communication has great impact on the ability of the hearing-impaired to participate in mainstream society." The Association President Arun Rao has cautioned that the hearing impaired people gradually become marginalized in the society. They should not be left unattended.

3

Communication with the Unseen

Lakhan Mehrotra

The history of human civilization as we know it from archaeological, epigraphic, literary and numismatic sources leads one to conclude that from times immemorial man has tried not only to communicate with his fellow beings but with a certain 'unseen' force which he could not see with eyes but whose presence he has felt way beyond the power of his ordinary senses. It is this power of extra sensory perception which makes him see reality beyond the limits of his senses and communicate with objects he cannot directly or immediately see with his eyes, touch with his fingers, taste with his tongue, smell with his nose or hear with his ears. In addition to his sensory capabilities, the human being has a remarkable faculty to look within, to turn the mind away from the objects of the world and explore several levels of consciousness that he finds lying within himself. He has tried to communicate with reality that thrives at those levels and then transmit the outcome to coming generations as he has done in respect of experiences born out of his contact with the objective world. Our Vedas and Upanishads were born thus as also some other 'revelations' that are contained in treatises of equally high renown such as the Bible and the Quran. They are the outcome of human endeavour to understand the reality of the world within and its relation to the world without, to see it with the mind's eye and to communicate with it through a variety of ways including intuition of which Mahatma Gandhi was so enamoured.

The exploration of the unseen through a discovery of the self and communication with it led our ancient sages, the Ṛishis, to conclude that there was an intrinsic connect between individual consciousness and cosmic consciousness and that in the ultimate analysis they were one and the same, not just inseparable but identical. This realization lay at the centre of their concept of the unity of all things. 'So'ham' (सोऽहम्)- I am He, 'Tattvamasi' (तत्त्वमसि)- That art thou, and 'Ahaṁ Brahmāsmi' (अहं ब्रह्मास्मि)- I myself am Brahmān are Vedic proclamations of that sense of one's identity with the Infinite. Sātvika (सात्विक) or pure knowledge is one, says Kṛishṇa in the *Bhagavadgītā*, that makes one see the same imperishable 'Bhāva' (भाव) or the real self in existence in all other beings as in oneself, the indivisible consciousness that inhabits all sentient beings which appear physically divided.[1]

In that view of life, the physical body is the temple of the soul. It is not the real self but its vehicle, its carrier, endowed with numerous faculties including the mind and the senses, both cognitive and motor, the *jñānendriyas* and the *karmendriyas*. The mind makes it possible for the human being to communicate with both – the self within and the universe without and is the cause of both its bondage and liberation.[2]

Communication with the self means realization of a truth that is subtler than both mind and the knowledge that it produces. It is also subtler than our physical frame. Communication with it age after age made the ancient seers realize that the real self within them was indeed not just their own but all pervasive. It was both the knower and the known. Every thing emanated from it and merged into it and nothing could exist without it. It is omnipresent and omnipotent. It is possible to communicate with it and to establish a communion with it. That is why the Upanishadic injunction: 'Ātma' or the self alọne is to be meditated upon, listened to and realized.[3]

There are many ways in which one may communicate with the self and establish a communion with it. It may be done through *bhakti*, the path of love and devotion; or *jñāna*, the path of knowledge; *dhyāna* or the path of meditation, and *karmayoga* or the path of selfless action. Those who follow the path of knowledge communicate with the Unseen as a 'reality' without form or attributes. *Bhakti* generally involves faith in God's Personal Being and surrender to His will but the *bhakta* may as well be a devotee of the formless and attributeless Ultimate Reality. One may also communicate with the Infinite through the path of selfless action, as duty rendered without any attachment to its fruit. Communication with the Unseen through meditation with the objective of realizing it and merging one's own self with it is *dhyānayoga*. Eventually all these paths lead one to the same goal, that is, self realization. People follow different paths in pursuing it according to their mental make-up and preferences.

A real *bhakta* is in constant communion with his Lord and seeks to do nothing that he feels is not in tune with His will. Says Kṛishṇa in the *Bhagavadgītā*:

> Through devotion one knows Me truly, how much and what I am.
>
> Then having known Me in my very essence forthwith enters Me.
>
> Performing all his deeds always taking refuge in Me
>
> Through My grace one attains My abode, eternal, imperishable.[4]

In this sequence of communicating with the Unseen, *bhakti* precedes *jñāna* and the latter precedes action done with a sense of surrender to the will of the Infinite, but these processes can be reversed or they may run concurrently. They do not exclude each other but are complimentary. However, the end result is the same: Yoga in each of these forms involves communicating with the Unseen, joining the 'individual' self with the 'Universal' self and realizing their identity, establishing the self in its eternal imperishable abode.

All prayer is an act of communication with the Unseen or the reality that is seen only with the inner eye. The Vedic Ṛishis felt its presence in the might and majesty of Nature and sought its bounties for the spiritual, mental and physical upkeep and progress of the human race. Vedic hymns comprise prayers to the infinite power that the Ṛishis saw lying at the very foundation of nature. They were the outcome of direct communication with it. They noticed that all the objects of Nature and its limitless domain, the cosmos, were governed by an abiding principle, the Ṛita, the Truth, that sustained order, both physical and moral, in the midst of constant flux and they sought its protection in their prayers. They also named it Brahman and bowed to it in prayer after realizing it as "the all pervading and all sustaining Truth or reality".[5] Says the *Ṛigveda*:

> In his prayers, his communication with Brahman – the Infinite and the indefinable Truth, the Ṛita, the Satya, the Vedic hymn

asked it to 'lead him from untruth to truth, darkness to light, and death to immortality'.[6]

That overarching principle, the Brahman, is 'unseen' because of its extreme subtlety. "It is so subtle it is both near to us and far away from us".[7] Says *Bhagavadgītā*:

> It is subtler than our intellect, which itself is subtler than the Manas, the mind which is subtler than the senses. What we can perceive through our senses (*indriyāṇi*) is very little as compared to our total experience. Even our mind is not the sole progenitor of the entire world of our experience. It is guided by the Buddhi intellect which discriminates between good and evil and makes us choose between right and wrong, institutes self-control in us and disallows the mind to be a prisoner of passions that generate tension and conflict. The intellect itself is constantly overseen by a subtler force within us, the Upadrishtā, the source of the 'inner voice' through which the seeker of the Truth communicates with the Ultimate Reality. This Ultimate is without beginning and without end; everything comes from it and goes into it. It is complete and total in itself all the time. All the mighty as well as tiny processes of Nature take place only within its realm and through all the cycles of creation, sustenance, destruction and resurgence its totality is never affected, it remains the same. In communicating with the Unseen the objective is to come face to face with that reality.

The Brahman is so subtle that it cannot be described as either existent or non-existent.[8] One can communicate with it only when the mind is rid of all *āvartta*s and *vivartta*s, volutes and convolutes – the sets of opposites or *dvandva*s which tear it into two, and of all thoughts and attachments which generate ripples and make it impossible to stabilize it.

Having attained that stability of mind, one descends into the realm of pure consciousness where one can communicate with the Unseen directly, 'see' it in all its grace and luminosity and realize it as Sachchidānanda, as Sat (Truth), Chit (Consciousness) and Ānanda (Joy). That experience comes when one transcends both the mind and the intellect and is consumed by the communion with the self. In that moment all communication, nay, one's entire existence dissolves into the cosmic, the Universal self. One's ego is gone. All barriers fall and all distinctions cease. One becomes Pureself. One is part of everyone and everything while centred in the Ultimate Reality.[9]

NOTES AND REFERENCES

1. सर्व भूतेषु येनैकं भावमव्ययमीक्षते।
   अविभद्रं विभद्रेषु तज्ज्ञानं विद्धि सात्त्विकम्।। 18.20
2. मन एव मनुष्याणां कारणं बन्धामोक्षयो:।।
3. आत्मैवारे मन्तव्य: श्रोतव्य: निधिाधयासितव्य:।
4. भक्त्या मामभिजानाति यावन्यश्चास्मि तत्वत:।
   ततो मां तत्त्वतो ज्ञात्वा विशते तदनन्तरम्।। 18.55
   सर्व कर्माण्यपि सदा कुर्वाणो मद्व्यपाश्रय:।
   मत्प्रसादादवाप्नोति शाश्वतं पदमव्ययम्।। 18.56
5. त्वमेव प्रत्यक्षं ब्रह्म वदिष्यामि ऋतं वदिष्यामि सत्यं वदिष्यामि
   तन्मामवतु तद्वद्रारमवतु अवतु मां अवतु वद्रारम्।।
6. असतो मा सद्गमय तमसो मा ज्योतिर्गमय मृत्योर्मामृतं गमयेति।।
7. सूक्ष्मत्वात्तद्विज्ञेयं दूरस्थं चान्तिके च तत्। 13.15
8. अनादिमत्परं ब्रह्म न सत्तन्नासदुच्यते। 13.12
9. सर्वथा वर्तमानोऽपि स योगी मयि वर्तते। 6.31

4

Extra Terrestrial Communication

K.N. Rao

In the age in which we live we do talk of visual and non-visual communication but rarely of extra terrestrial communication that leaves those who experience it and know, absolutely dazzled and makes them wonder why they did not pay more attention to it earlier. It is because, as a scientist said, man has not conquered nature but nature in some graceful moments has yielded some of her secrets to man.

Communications as understood in these days clearly means a link up physically between two ends, one the communicating original place and the other the receiving end. In these days of proliferating media, electronic particularly, it is transmission and reception in simple language.

Such communication has always existed whether it is physical, terrestrial or cosmic or extra terrestrial since Creation. But the dominance of physical sciences and technology has diminished and even ridiculed and rejected extra terrestrial communications.

In scriptures lives of prophets and saints speak of divine messages which can be from sublime to ridiculous, uplifting to dangerous, elevating to destructive as human history shows. But there are other areas where one has to learn the art of understanding the extra terrestrial message or signals given by nature, flora and fauna, animals and of course planets and eclipses.

OMENS

In all religious traditions, there is mention of omens, good or evil, as being indicative of some future happening. There is not a single religious book of the Hindus, whether it is the *Vālmīkīya Rāmāyaṇa,* the *Mahābhārata* or the *Purāṇas*, where they are not referred to. These are treated as communications from good to ominous and taken seriously. Can modern man ignore it? See for instance, what Lord Rāma himself says: "Seeing the omens it is certain that I will kill Ravana and bring back Sītā.[1]

Or see again,

"Man gets indications of his happiness through omens, dreams, from birds, from svara (breath) etc." for those who do not take it seriously, I must state here that I have had occasions to write thrice about it in connection with Indian elections or tragedies.[2]

RAJIV GANDHI'S DEATH

On 21 May 1991, there was an unusually violent shower and hail in Delhi at about five in the evening and four hours later we heard about the assassination of Rajiv Gandhi.

END OF P.V. NARASIMHA RAO'S CAREER

In 1996, P.V. Narasimha Rao went to address an election rally in his constituency but a terrible torrential downpour of rain forced him to seek protection under the wing of an aeroplane and not address the meeting. His political career ended from that day when he was not given a party ticket to fight election.

LALU LOSES BIHAR

Similarly, Lalu Prasad Yadav was addressing election meetings in Bihar and twice the stage on which he stood collapsed and he lost power as the Chief Minister of Bihar.

Such instances are noticed, privately commented on by many people who know the importance of *nimitta*s but are not collected and accepted by the physical scientists who would dismiss them as superstitions.

There are extra terrestrial communications known since ages to mankind are generally part of folklore and not a subject of serious study in modern universities.

The danger of not studying all this phenomena systematically, analyzing them, producing a statistical study, making an advanced prediction on their basis always leads to the danger to reducing all these into dangerous superstitions as happens mostly in India.

For instance, Indian astrologers who make lot of money through the fraudulent Kala Sarpa Yoga, can never show a single astrological classic where it is mentioned and there is no study of this but it is a money spinner. It survives because it is lucrative for astrologers to frighten their clients. Same happens when omens are not studied systematically and interpreted superstitiously. This lurking danger must always be kept in the mind.

MONSOON AND NATURE AND PLANETS

It is and has been in the forecasting of the Indian monsoon, since India has been a predominantly an agricultural country depended on the south-west monsoon for seventy per cent of its needs for water, that India has had a long tradition of depending on extra terrestrial phenomena to see the nature of the coming rains. The Indian Meteorological Department failed to forecast the drought of 2002 and the good rains of 2003 while astrologically it was predicted months in advance accurately (see appendix one). Let it be illustrated here with an example first and later explained in a layman's language.

GUJARAT EARTHQUAKE OF 26 JANUARY 2001 (FROM FEBRUARY 11TH ISSUE OF THE WEEK MAGAZINE) FATAL FEBRUARY!

A catastrophe in store for north India, says astrologer who predicted the quake

February will prove to be a bad month for north India, says noted astrologer K.N. Rao.

Rao has made many correct predictions including the assassination of Prime Minister Indira Gandhi in 1984. In *The Week* dated January 14, 2001, he said, "The country will face crippling natural calamities." He was the least surprised when the massive earthquake rocked Gujarat on Republic Day.

Rao predicts cyclones, earthquakes and other natural calamities on the basis of Varahamihira's *Brihajjataka,* a classic written in the fifth century. He also uses certain Rajasthani manuscripts. For predicting the Gujarat earthquake, Rao considered the lunar eclipse in the first week of January and the new Hindu year Chaitra Shukla Pratipada, besides the planetary positions.

NORTH INDIAN EARTHQUAKE

See further what happened in northern India *Times of India,* 26 Feb. 2001

NORTH INDIA ROCKED; BUT NO DAMAGE REPORTED

New Delhi: An earthquake measuring 6.7 on the Richter scale rocked northern India and parts of Central Asia on Sunday morning with people rushing out of their houses in panic.

The quake was experienced in Delhi, Punjab, Haryana, parts of Rajasthan, Jammu and Kashmir and Chandigarh.

THE BASIS

These are cases of interpreting the extra terrestrial messages based on using eclipses (remember the eclipses of January 2001) and the changing of the motions of two major planets, Jupiter and Saturn.

That terrible earthquake of 26 January 2001 could not have been predicted except through the methods given to us by Ṛishi Gargacharya and Varahamihira because it has been and will remain beyond the range and techniques of seismologists all over the world.

Such methods of interpreting extra terrestrial messages forged into predictive tools but neglected is what man has to pay for heavily in the present and coming decades, particularly in the year 2007-2008 the years of manmade and natural disasters.

DROUGHT OF 1987

In the *Panchanga* of Venkateshwara Press (published in 1944 and available in the market) a couplet in Hindi was quoted:

> Shravan me aage chala Ravirath se Kujaray
> Bhadon Kṛishṇa pakhlo varsha svalpa dikhahi.

It is an unbelievable forecast of the drought of 1987 given forty-three years in advance based on of the movement of planets, Mars and Sun and further, a more remarkable prediction that it would rain scantily till the dark lunar fortnight of Bhadra Masa or August. It was only after first 20th August and later after the 28th that the drought situation was overcome though it was too late.

But will reality of such proofs break rudely ever into the nightmarish limitations of physical scientists who have closed their eyes to effect or extra terrestrial phenomena with more obstinate prejudice and ignorance and without any proper understanding, intelligence and interpretation? It will shake the shaky, now vulnerable fortresses of physical scientists who monopolise and grab all the funds and funding all over the world. Why continue to grope in the dark and allow humanity to suffer?

LIMITATIONS OF SEISMOLOGISTS

Seismologists have studied the areas where here can be seismological shocks but are so totally ignorant of its occurrence that their guess can have range of one year to ten years. Astrologers working on earthquakes, full and new Moon see the timing more closely, but even the astrological research has not reached a point of infallibility. If both, the terrestrial and the extra terrestrial are combined the benefit humanity can have so immense. See a typical case reported on 25 April 2007. See the forecast of a physical scientist.

MASSIVE QUAKE LIKELY ON INDO-BHUTAN BORDER: GSI

PTI! Ultapani (Assam)

There is a possibility of a massive earthquake striking the Indo-Bhutan border in Assam in the near future, a senior scientist of the Geological Survey of India has said. K. Mazumdar of GSI currently heading a study team on earthquake alerts, today informed that a "quake with a magnitude of more than seven on the Richter scale could hit the area on the foothills of Bhutan in Assam's Kokrajhar district and it might extend north up to Kamrup district".

NOTHING THAT IT WAS DIFFICULT TO PREDICT THE TIME OF SUCH A QUAKE.

Mazumdar speaks of the difficulty of timing because he will never use, being prejudiced, the extra terrestrial communications given by planets and eclipses on which astrologers have based their stray, yet successful, forecasts of earthquakes.

EXTRA TERRESTRIAL COMMUNICATION IS INFORMATION

Since ancient times man had to study signals from nature as his pieces of information. Other than planets, we can turn our attention to flora and fauna and birds and animals as communicating what man can use of. See some instances.

A plant in Himachal Pradesh known as *nag phana* begins to fade out early if there is going to be drought. Looking at the plant, the farmers of Himachal Pradesh had predicted in 1987 the year long drought before the meteorologists realized that the country was in the grip of a drought which the Prime Minister Rajiv Gandhi talked of so vociferously to divert the attention of the nation from the Bofors scandal.

In all these types of communication man has to develop skill to interpret, understand and in turn pass on the information so received to his fellow human beings. In a way, it is a one sided communication because Nature has conveyed, given advanced information about a future happening which in terms of time is immediate, short range, medium range and long range.

In the technologically advanced, the total derision and negligence of such extra terrestrial communication has led to their failure to predict the disaster of 16 October 1987 (see appendix II)

Interestingly, when the Indian nation waited with abated breath to find out who would be the UPA candidate for the post of the president of India, no one knew or expected Srimati Pratibha Patil to be the final choice. But it was predicted to her (see appendix III). That is astral or extra terrestrial communication and an instance like this keeps faith in astrology alive in India in spite of many failures to predict.

Hundreds of such instances can be given but we can still not have a deep satisfaction from such instances as this method understanding extra terrestrial communications should be studied statistically by taking up many cases which cannot be done by a single astrologer. A team of well trained astrologers if made to work after attractive remuneration over a period of time, will surely succeed in producing a most dependable of interpreting these signals and turn them into most dependable tool for prediction for humanity it may happen in future decades as an effort in this direction has begun and has been succeeding.

The inevitable conclusion has to be that Nature will remain a grand mystery sending out communications which man has tried to understand, interpret and, on this basis, predict future. Yet, Nature must remain a many splendoured mystery yielding some of her secrets gracefully sometimes and never all her secrets.

APPENDIX I

(बरसेंगे जमकर मेघदूत)

वर्ष 2003 भविष्यवाणी

अगर किसी ज्योतिषी से पूछा जाय कि 2003 में बरसात कैसी होगी तो उत्तर होगा अच्छी - सामान्य से अधिक। अगर पूछा जाय कि जुलाई में जिस महीने की बरसात पर कृषक निर्भर करते है कैसी होगी तो फिर उत्तर होगा अच्छी सामान्य से अधिक। किन्तु मौसम विभाग ने शायद पहली बार मानसून के बारे में ऐसी निराशाजनक भविष्यवाणी की है।

दैनिक भास्कर के सौजन्य से रविवार 4 मई, 2003

Finally it turned out that the year 2003 was a year of good monsoon which the meteorologists failed to see but could be seen easily astrologically.

APPENDIX II

On October 16th, 1987 when a hurricane devastated London, the *Daily Telegraph* of October 17th, 1987 reported:

"The Meteorological office has launched an inquiry to establish why it failed to forecast the severity of gales."

The editorial comment of the *Daily Telegraph* on October 17th, 1987 was "The British weather in 1987 appears to be exhausting its capacity to astonish us, it is part of our contemporary enthusiasm for self mockery that we deride our own incompetence in coping with a gale as we did in the face of the upsets caused by last January's blizzards. Yet all that has changed over the century is the nature of our vulnerability and the growth of arrogance concerning our capacity to tame acts of God. Post-Darwinian high technological confidence offers different explanation, but still no solution."

If astrologers had worked on this they would have seen that:

a) In January 1987, Mercury on 12th and 27th January and Mars and Rāhu in the last week of January 1987 caused it.

b) On October 16th, 1987 the astrological phenomenon on the basis of which Indian astrologers had warned of such disaster, though not mentioning England specifically, was the retrogression of Mercury and Mars. Rāhu aspects mutually and very closely. It was on this basis that I had predicted that Reliance Cup matches would be affected by uncertain weather. The same principle could have been extended to England particularly (here comes in an instance of coordination between the astrologer and the meteorologist) when a depression was forming in the mid-Atlantic dictated by satellite.

APPENDIX III

http://www.hindustantimes.com/StoryPage/FullcoverageStorypage.aspx?id=e952a457-b4d5-41fb-936b-b5

Soft-spoken but aggressive

Pratibha Patil is UPA nominee for president's post June 14, 2007

Dharmendra Jore, *Hindustan Times*

Mumbai, June 14, 2007

Last Updated: 16:27 IST (15/6/2007)

Last year, an astrologer told Pratibha Patil that she wouldn't complete her term as the Rajasthan Governor, and instead she would move out to occupy a more important post in near future.

Patil's husband Devisingh Shekhawat said the prediction was all set to come true. "Then we didn't take the prediction seriously. But now, I can't restrain myself from making it public", he said.

NOTES AND REFERENCES

1. *Vālmīkīya Rāmāyaṇa, Yuddha Kāṇḍa*, 4.6.
   निमित्तानि च पश्यामि यानि प्रादुर्भवन्ति वै। निहत्य रावणं सीतामानयिश्यामि जानकीम्।।
2. Ibid., *Araṇya Kāṇḍa*, 52.2.
   निमित्तं लक्षणं स्वप्नं शकुनिस्वरदर्शनम्। अवश्यं सुखदुःखेषु नराणां परिदृश्यते।।

5

मृत्यु से संबंधित कुछ खास प्रश्न-उत्तर
(श्री उपेन्द्र वाजपेयी और आचार्य महाप्रज्ञ के प्रश्नोतर)

आचार्य महाप्रज्ञ

प्रश्न 1: मृत्यु की परिभाषा क्या होगी?

उत्तर : स्थूल शरीर और प्राण का वियोग होने पर जीव और सूक्ष्मतम शरीर (कर्म शरीर) के संयुक्त प्रयत्न के द्वारा नए जीवन के प्रारंभ में संयोग (जीवनी शक्ति) का निर्माण होता है। उसका काम है बाहर से पुद्गलों का ग्रहण, शरीर के रूप में परिणमन और उसका रेचन। जीवनी शक्ति प्राण का स्रोत है। उसकी क्रिया जब समाप्त होती है और प्राण ऊर्जा का स्रोत सूख जाता है, वही है मृत्यु।

प्रश्न 2: जब शरीर निर्जीव हो जाए, प्राणविहीन हो जाए - अगर, शरीर से प्राण चला जाए, इसका अर्थ है शरीर में पहले प्राण था - यदि अब चला गया तो कहां गया?

उत्तर : प्राण स्थूल शरीर से पृथक् होकर आकाशमंडल में चले जाते हैं। वे एक सीमित समय तक मुक्त शरीर के आकाश में भी रह सकते हैं और उसके बाद उनका रूपान्तरण हो जाता है।

प्रश्न 3: जब यह कहा गया है कि मृत्यु शरीर की होती है, आत्मा की नहीं, तो शरीर की मृत्यु होने पर आत्मा कहां चली जाती है?

उत्तर : 'मृत्यु शरीर की होती है', यह सापेक्ष वाक्य है। 'मृत्यु आत्मा की होती है' यह भी सापेक्ष वाक्य है। वास्तविकता यह है कि प्राण ऊर्जा की शक्ति समाप्त होने पर शरीर पड़ा रहता है और आत्मा किसी स्थान पर चली जाती है।

प्रश्न 4: क्या सब आत्माएं एक ही जगह जाती हैं या अलग-अलग? इसका निर्णय कौन करता है? आत्मा के निवास की पुष्टि किस भांति की जा सकती है?

उत्तर : वर्तमान जीवन में भावी जीवन का स्थान अपने-अपने कर्म के अनुरूप निर्धारित हो जाता है। मृत्यु के बाद आत्मा निर्धारित स्थान पर चली जाती है। यह सारी प्रक्रिया चेतना और सूक्ष्म शरीर के योग से सम्पादित होती है।

प्रश्न 5: 'न जायते म्रियते वा कदाचिन्, नायं भूत्वा भविता वा न भूयः'[1]। यदि यह सही है तो आत्मा के होने या चले जाने का प्रश्न ही नहीं उठता। फिर, आत्मा की रूपरेखा क्या होगी? या, आत्मा की कल्पना ही दोषपूर्ण है?

उत्तर : * 'न जायते म्रियते वा कदाचिन्, नायं भूत्वा भविता वा न भूयः' यह सिद्धांत शरीर मुक्त आत्मा यानी सूक्ष्म शरीर से भी मुक्त आत्मा के लिए प्रतिपादित है।

* आत्मा चैतन्यमय असंख्य प्रदेशों - परमाणुओं का अविभक्त समुदाय है।

प्रश्न 6: प्राण और आत्मा एक ही हैं या दोनों की सत्ता अलग है?

उत्तर : प्राण और आत्मा भिन्न हैं। प्राण पौद्गलिक शक्ति है और आत्मा चेतन है। आत्मा के द्वारा प्रत्येक जीवन में प्राण-ऊर्जा का निर्माण किया जाता है।

प्रश्न 7: प्राण का बोध तो मनुष्य को अनेक प्रकार से होता रहता है - सांस चलना, हृदय धड़कना, देखना, सुनना, अन्य इन्द्रियों की क्रिया, इसी प्रकार क्या आत्मा के चरित्र को पहचानना संभव है?

उत्तर : प्राण के द्वारा श्वास का संचालन होता है। श्वास और श्वास-प्राण दो हैं। जिस शक्ति के द्वारा श्वास लिया जाता है वह श्वास प्राण है और जो ऑक्सीजन ग्रहण किया जाता है वह श्वास है।
प्राण के द्वारा पूर्ण शरीर का संचालन होता है इसे स्वीकार करने में कोई कठिनाई नहीं है।

प्रश्न 8: आत्मा यदि सूक्ष्म है जिसे इन्द्रियों से नहीं पहचाना जा सकता तो आत्मा के बोध का निरूपण किस प्रकार होगा?

उत्तर : अधिकांश व्यक्ति आत्मा का बोध शास्त्रों के माध्यम से करते हैं। बहुत कम व्यक्ति ऐसे हैं, जो अपनी ध्यान-समाधि के द्वारा चेतना

के सूक्ष्म स्पन्दनों को पकड़ लेते हैं और आत्मानुभूति के क्षण में चले जाते हैं। दार्शनिक सिद्धांत यह है कि केवल ज्ञान की स्थिति में अमूर्त आत्मा का भी साक्षात्कार हो सकता है।

प्रश्न 9: गीता में श्रीकृष्ण ने कहा है – 'जातस्य हि ध्रुवो मृत्युः ध्रुवं जन्म मृतस्य च'[2]। पहले का प्रमाण तो नित्य मिलता रहता है, चाहे हम मृत्यु को जिस प्रकार परखना चाहें, किंतु 'ध्रुवं जन्म मृतस्य च' – इसे कुछ इने गिने उदाहरणों को छोड़कर जिनमें मनुष्य अपने पूर्वजन्म की याद करता है, कैसे कहा जा सकता है 'ध्रुवं जन्म मृतस्य च'?

उत्तर : पुनर्जन्म का सिद्धांत कुछ व्यक्तियों की स्मृति पर ही अवलंबित नहीं है। उसका दार्शनिक और आध्यात्मिक आधार है। प्रत्यक्ष के आधार पर नहीं कहा जा सकता कि आत्मा, परमात्मा अथवा मोक्ष है, किन्तु दार्शनिक और तार्किक आधार पर आत्मा का सिद्धांत स्थापित है। विश्व का कोई भी तत्व सर्वथा नष्ट नहीं होता, केवल पर्याय का परिवर्तन होता है। पर्याय परिवर्तन के आधार पर 'ध्रुवं जन्म मृतस्य च' यह स्वीकार करना कोई समस्या नहीं है।

प्रश्न 10: यदि जन्म और मृत्यु का रहस्य अभी रहस्य ही है तो क्या यह कहा जा सकता है कि जितने धर्मोपदेश हैं, उनका मुख्य उद्येश्य समाज को यथासंभव व्यवस्थित-शांतिपूर्ण बनाए रखना है, इसलिए कुछ आस्थाएं गढ़ी गयी हैं?

उत्तर : समाज को व्यवस्थित शांतिपूर्ण बनाए रखने के लिए यदि धर्मोपदेश है तो उसे सामाजिक उपयोगिता से अधिक महत्व नहीं दिया जा सकता, किन्तु हमारी दृष्टि में धर्म का आधार-बिन्दु है अतीन्द्रिय-चेतना। इन्द्रिय चेतना पर आधारित धर्म को सामाजिक मूल्य का नाम दिया जा सकता है, किन्तु अतीन्द्रिय चेतना के आधार पर निर्मित धर्म की आचार-संहिता को केवल उपयोगिता की कोटि में नहीं रखा जा सकता।

प्रश्न 11: क्या यह सही है कि धर्म की जितनी कल्पनाएं हैं, वे पारलौकिक नहीं, यथार्थ में इहलौकिक ही हैं?

उत्तर : धर्माचरण के द्वारा वर्तमान जीवन में पवित्रता आती है इसीलिए वह इहलौकिक भी है और उससे भविष्य में होने वाला जन्म भी अच्छा होता है इसलिए वह पारलौकिक भी है।

प्रश्न 12: क्या उन्हें पारलौकिक बनाने का उद्देश्य केवल मनुष्य में किसी अदृश्य, अगोचर, शक्ति के प्रति आस्था जगाकर उसे (मनुष्य) अधिक 'सामाजिक' या 'समाजप्रिय' बनाना है? 'ईश्वर' की कल्पना भी क्या इसी प्रकार की है? वास्तविकता यह है कि दृश्य से अदृश्य अधिक शक्तिमान सिद्ध हुआ है - दैनिक जीवन में भी।

उत्तर : जन-साधारण में शक्ति के प्रति आकर्षण होता है। शक्ति केन्द्र दृश्य और अदृश्य दोनों हो सकते हैं। अदृश्य अधिक आकर्षण का केन्द्र इसलिए बनता है कि उसमें काल्पनिक शक्ति का आरोपण भी किया जा सकता है।

प्रश्न 13: मृत शरीर के अंतिम संस्कार की विधि विभिन्न धर्मों, संप्रदायों में अलग अलग है। इससे क्या मृतक की अंतिम यात्रा पर कोई अंतर पड़ने की संभावना है?

उत्तर : अंतिम संस्कार की विधि का मृतक की आत्मा पर प्रभाव होना कोई अनिवार्य नियम नहीं है।

प्रश्न 14: यदि मृत्यु के बाद मनुष्य पंचतत्व में विलीन हो जाता है तो क्या यह समझा जा सकता है कि उसके चित्र, साहित्य, दर्शन या अवगुणों के रूप में उसकी स्मृति के अतिरिक्त कुछ भी शेष नहीं रहता[3]?

उत्तर : मृत्यु के बाद परिचित व्यक्तियों में स्मृति के अतिरिक्त कुछ नहीं रहता, यह स्वीकार करने में कोई कठिनाई नहीं है। कुछ मृत आत्माओं का पारिवारिकजनों के साथ सम्पर्क स्थापित हो सकता है। वह सहज भी हो सकता है और प्रयत्नपूर्वक भी हो सकता है।

प्रश्न 15: बुद्ध, महावीर, गांधी जैसे कुछ अपवादों को छोड़कर स्मृति भी अधिकांश की विलीन होती जाती है।

उत्तर : स्मृति का संबंध विशेष घटनाओं और विशेष अवदानों के साथ है। इसलिए उन्हीं लोगों की स्मृति रहती है, जिनका कार्य उत्कर्ष के बिन्दु तक पहुंच जाता है। भले फिर वह कार्य अच्छा हो या अच्छा न हो।

प्रश्न 16: जिनकी स्मृति लंबे समय तक बनी रहती है, उनके कर्तृत्व और आदर्शों को लोग भूल जाते हैं। बस उनका नाम याद रखते हैं और समय-समय पर फूलमाला चढ़ाकर समझ लेते हैं अपना कर्त्तव्य पूरा कर लिया, चाहे नित्य जीवन में उनका आचरण अपने 'आराध्य' के सर्वथा विपरीत हो?

उत्तर : पूजा करना जितना सरल कार्य है, आचरण उतना सरल नहीं है। इस सचाई को हम कभी विस्मृत न करें।

प्रश्न 17: इस परिस्थिति में क्या यह कहना उचित नहीं होगा कि ईश्वर-भक्ति, धर्म या तथाकथित आस्था का स्थान वास्तव में पाखंड[4] ने ले लिया है?

उत्तर : 'पाखंड' शब्द का विश्लेषण करना कठिन है। आस्था और आचरण की दूरी को मिटाने का प्रयत्न नहीं किया जाता इसलिए आस्था कहीं-कहीं पाखंड का रूप ले भी सकती है।

प्रश्न 18: निश्चय ही कुछ विशिष्ट व्यक्ति ऐसे हैं जो 'स्वधर्मे निधनं श्रेय:'[5] मानकर धर्मपरायण बने रहते हैं। किंतु शासन, प्रशासन, मीडिया सर्वत्र ऐसे लोगों की संख्या बढ़ती जा रही है जो अपनी सुख-सुविधा के लिए सभी प्रकार की मान्यताओं को तिलांजलि देते जा रहे हैं?

उत्तर : जितने तथाकथित बड़े लोग हैं, वे किसी भी क्षेत्र के हों, उनके लिए मृत्यु के बाद होने वाले जन्म की कल्पना करना संभवत: अपेक्षित नहीं है। उन पर वर्तमान के वैभव का इतना अधिक प्रभाव होता है कि सुदूर भविष्य की उनकी चेतना मूर्च्छित हो जाती है। बुद्धि हमेशा भावना से प्रभावित होती है। 'न चायुक्तस्य भावना'[6] इस सचाई की हम अपेक्षा नहीं कर सकते।

प्रश्न 19 से 22:

आप ही के शब्दों में ऊपर के कुछ 'वैभवशाली' लोगों को छोड़कर जो बीस और पचीस करोड़ के बीच होंगे - शेष की अवस्था अच्छी नहीं है। लगभग चालीस करोड़ भुखमरों की श्रेणी में हैं।

क्या जाने-अनजाने इस देश के कर्णधार और उच्च वर्ग के लोग हिंसक क्रांति को निमंत्रण दे रहे हैं? वह कितनी अनिष्टकारी हो सकती है इसका अहसास कितनों को है कोई कह सकता है?

आप जैसे महापुरूष हिंसा और लोलुपता की बाढ़ की रोकथाम के लिए बांध बना रहे है, पर यह हाहाकारी बाढ़ को रोकने में कितना समर्थ होगा?

आपकी यह सम्मति, आपका उपदेश सौ फीसदी सही है कि हम अपना कर्त्तव्य करते रहें। किंतु, कर्त्तव्य करने वालों को यह प्रतीत होने लगे कि वे समाज की धारा सुधार नहीं पा रहे हैं तो क्या होगा?

व्यवहार में अनेक बार देखा गया है कि असफलता अथवा अपेक्षित सफलता न प्रतीत होने पर अपने नज़दीकी लोग भी साथ छोड़ देते हैं। आपके ही शब्दों में स्वाधीनता आंदोलन में जो 'समग्र सहयोग' इस देश में अथवा अन्य देशों में देखा गया वह अन्य उद्देश्यों के लिए साधारणतया संभव नहीं है।

इसके अतिरिक्त वास्तविक या कल्पित स्वार्थों/मतान्तरों का टकराव हो जाता है। आज संसार में जितने संप्रदाय या राजनीतिक गिरोह हैं, वे इसी के प्रतिबिंब कहे जा सकते हैं। परिणाम क्या है?

उत्तर : इस देश के कर्णधार हिंसक क्रांति को निमंत्रण दे रहे हैं। सीधे-सीधे यह कहना आरोप हो सकता है। किन्तु सचाई को अस्वीकार करना आरोप से अधिक अन्याय है। यदि देश के कर्णधार मूलभूत समस्याओं के प्रति जागरूक हों तो वे हिंसक क्रांति की संभावना को बदल सकते हैं।

मेरा अभिमत है कि देश के कर्णधारों के पास इतना चरित्रबल नहीं है और इतना पारमार्थिक दृष्टिकोण भी नहीं है कि वे हिंसक क्रांति के तूफान की दिशा को मोड़ सकें।

अहिंसा में निष्ठा रखने वाले व्यक्ति, संस्थाएं और सरकार सहभागिता के सिद्धांत पर कार्य करें तो समस्या की तीव्रता को कम किया जा सकता है।

NOTES AND REFERENCES

1. *Bhagavadgītā*, 2.20.
2. Ibid., 2.27.
3. चार्वाक के "यावज्जीवेत सुखं जीवेत... भस्मीभूतस्य देहस्य पुनरागमनं कुतः" का भौतिकतावादी सिद्धान्त और बुद्ध का अनात्मवादी पुद्गल-शून्यता का सिद्धान्त-दोनों की आत्मा के अस्तित्व को नकारते थे किन्तु 'तथता' के सिद्धान्त द्वारा बुद्ध पुनर्जन्म की बात करते थे जिसे चार्वाक ने नकारा था। (रा.वा.)
4. छठी शताब्दी ईस्वी पूर्व में बुद्ध के नैतिकतावादी 'धाम्म' के विरोधियों ने उसे पाषण्ड (पाखंड) या दिखावा कहा था। बुद्ध ने वैदिक यज्ञ विरोधी सभी नैतिकतावादी सिद्धान्तों को पाषण्ड की संज्ञा दी थी। अशोक ने अपने लेखों में पाषण्ड शब्द का प्रयोग किया था। (रा. वा.)
5. *Bhagavadgītā*, 3.35.
6. Ibid., 2.66.

6

Communication in Prehistoric Period

S.P. Gupta

INTRODUCTION

The method of communication of any message from one individual to the other has a hoary past. Also, it is not confined to human beings, animals also communicate. Irish scientists monitoring dolphins believe they may have developed a unique dialect to communicate with each other. "We are building up a catalogue of the different whistle types they use and trying to associate them with behaviour like foraging, resting, socialising and the communications of groups with calves", project leader Simon Berrow said. "Essentially we are building up what is like a dictionary of words they use or sounds they make." "They do a whole range of barks, groans and a kind of gunshot", he said.

Apes too communicate as the recent studies on chimpanzees have amply proved – they use hands, palms, facial changes, and, of course, howlers and whispers of many kinds to make it effective. Since chimpanzees are closest to human beings in anatomy and behavioural pattern, anthropologists feel that the humans may also have been resorting to these techniques of communication.

However, from around 20,000-14000 years ago humans are seen doing paintings and making engravings on the walls of the caves they lived in, and also carving statuettes in bone, ivory and stone. More than 20,000 years ago, the prehistoric humans in India also, particularly in Rajasthan, as at *Dharti ka Chattan*, had been carving out cup-like marks on the surface of the rock-shelters, generally on walls. All these are believed to be methods of communication. Since such works of Rock Art are found also in

Africa, Southern Europe, as well as in Russia, Australia, USA, and many other parts of the world it is amply clear that these were not meant exclusively for self-satisfaction, i.e. art for art sake, but to communicate and share coming plan for hunting-and-gathering, i.e. economic efforts for which mobilization of human beings was essential, such as killing a mammoth (an elephant) or gathering edible wild roots or collecting honey.

On grounds of ethno-archaeological studies, scholars have also come to realise that a group of this art was certainly magico-religious in intent and purpose. It is, therefore, probable, that these were equally meant to communicate and share ideas and beliefs concerning supernatural powers. The statuettes of 'mother goddesses' belong to yet another category by which the ideas of fertility and procreation where conveyed to the fellow-beings. Then there are stone-pieces bearing linear motifs. They were carried from one place to another. Hence, yet another mode of communication in the stone ages. There may have been, of course, other methods also, but their archaeological evidence is not easy to find.

ROCK ART IN INDIA: MEDIUM OF COMMUNICATION BY PREHISTORIC HUMANS

The term 'Rock Art' is generally used for the prehistoric art, belonging mainly to the Stone Age, although in many regions it continued in the historical periods as well. Since, in the Stone Age human beings depended for their supply of food primarily on hunting animals and other creatures as well as gathering fruits, vegetables, edible roots, honey, etc. the art mainly depicts themes centring round these items. This art generally includes representations of wild animals, individually or in groups, stationary or fleeing, usually shown being hunted by human beings. However, there are also the representations of the floral world as well as geometric forms. This vast variety of motifs and themes picked from daily life and environment was rarely exclusive to each site; by and large these are found repeated in one form or other at very many places; on a regional basis their distribution has been worked out by several scholars. Their meaning is, therefore, clear – everyone in the region understood them in terms of intent and purpose. This happen to be the earliest evidence on communication in prehistoric times.

VARIOUS KINDS OF ROCK ART AND THEIR IMPORTANCE IN COMMUNICATION METHODOLOGIES

The Rock Art includes (i) paintings done in caves and rock-shelters as well as on open-air boulders, (ii) engravings etched in linear forms on rock surfaces, irrespective of their formations and location, (iii) peckings carried out on rock surfaces in clusters of dots making different forms, men, animal and geometric, (iv) cup-marks or cupulas created on rock surfaces in the form of deep or shallow roundels, and (v) carvings, leading to works of art in relief, or else in the round, done on pieces of bone, stone and ivory as well as large rock surfaces. Although all these categories, and a few more, are important, the largest number of them account for paintings which are found in many parts of the world – India, Africa, Southern Europe, Russia, America, Australia, and Asia. Many of these works of art were discovered during the last two decades of the nineteenth century and the first half of the twentieth century; but these are still being discovered all over the world. In India these were first discovered by John Cockburn and A. Carlleyle in the Vindhyan ranges of Banda and Mirzapur Districts. Much work was done in the late twentieth century by S.K. Pandey, Jagdish Gupta, Giriraj Kumar, besides V.S. Wakankar, Manoranjan Ghosh, D.H. Gordon, V.N. Misra and several others of the past generations. All these explorers and excavators had come to realize that it was a global phenomenon and that it had the element of communication of ideas by some one to the other.

DISTRIBUTION AND CHRONOLOGY OF ROCK ART COMMUNICATION METHODS: EUROPE AND INDIA

Of the most famous prehistoric rock paintings located outside India are those of Altamira caves located in Spain, and Lascaux caves located in France. In India, the ones in the Vindhyan rock-shelters of Bhimbethka are outstanding due to which the entire site has been included in the "World Heritage Site" by the UNESCO. However, similar paintings are found at Adamgarh near Hoshangabad on the Narmadā in Madhya Pradesh and at Lekhaniā in Mirzapur, Uttar Pradesh. There are, of course, many more rock-shelters in the Kaimur ranges in central India also-so also in Tamil Nadu, Karnataka, Andhra Pradesh, Kerala, Orissa and Gujarat.

While the earliest prehistoric paintings of Europe are generally dated to the Upper Palaeolithic period, starting from the times of the Aurignacian Culture, going back to the period from 33,000 BCE, this tradition continued up to the end of the Pleistocene Period or the Glacial Age almost 10,000 BCE. The Indian ones, however, start only around 8000-5000 BCE time-bracket, belonging to the Mesolithic period – but they continue till almost the end of the eighteenth century CE. Whether or not some paintings belong to the Upper Palaeolithic times is difficult to say in the present state of our knowledge.

BHIMBETHKĀ: THE INDIAN WORLD HERITAGE PREHISTORIC SITE

Discovered in 1957 by V.S. Wakankar, the rock-shelters of Bhịmbethkā, located in Distt. Raisen of Madhya Pradesh, are only 50 km from Bhopal. Like many other rock-shelter paintings, most of the paintings at Bhimbethkā are found done in different shades of red -from deep brown to yellowish red. However, black, yellow and white are also used extensively; only sometimes colours like green and blue are found used. The paints used are invariably non-organic, i.e. mineral or products of minerals or earth-produced ochres. The most popularly used mineral is brown-coloured haematite, which is iron-based and found in nature in various forms of nodules, some in the form of pencils. Copper-bearing pyrites were also used to produce green, but only occasionally. Calcium-based nodules, such as *kaikars*, produced various shades of white and dull yellow. Carbon was used to produce black. The colours were generally mixed with water, natural glues, blood and animal fats.

The paintings were executed directly on the exposed surfaces of the rocks; there was no preparation of the ground with any kind of paste of clay or lime to make the surface plain and smooth to make paintings on, as was done at Ajantā in the historical times. The colours, therefore, entered into the pores of the coarse surface of the rocks. The rocks are either a variety of sandstone formations, or their metamorphosed forms like quartzite; the other formations, i.e. those of the igneous rocks, for example, granite, basalt or gabbros, mainly in south India and the Deccan, are found only rarely used for executing paintings, although engravings and peckings are found executed on them very often, particularly during the Neolithic period and later in the historical times.

The paintings are done either in lines or outlines, some filled in with hatched lines, the others filled in fully or partially in solid colours.

The pictures, sometimes covering large spaces, are usually filled with multiple figures of humans and animals. However, small and large individual figures of men, women and animals are also found depicted in the rock-shelters of not only India but also Africa, Australia and other countries.

DATING THE ROCK ART IN INDIA: CHALLENGES AND SOLUTIONS

These paintings are often found superimposed by paintings done in later periods, without any regard to the pre-existing paintings. It is thus not very easy to separate them periodwise although some sequences have been made out by applying the method of "later ones override the earlier ones", i.e. stratigraphy. However, in India, since some paintings depict the scenes found on the potteries of the Chalcolithic period of the second millennium BCE, these are dated to that period. Similarly, some paintings carry inscriptions in the Mauryan-Sungan Brāhmi, thus these are dated to the period bracketed between 300 BCE and CE 50. There are then pictures of marriages in which costumes as well as the weapons depicted belong stylistically to the eighteenth century. In this way attempts have been made by some scholars to date them to various time-frames. However, physical and chemical methods of dating, such as the radiocarbon and AMS methods, have also been used but only rarely, generally in some foreign countries, such as Australia, where white paint has been dated, but their results are more or less tentative. In recent years, it has been claimed, generally on the basis of stratigraphy, that the cup-marks in India as well as elsewhere belong to the Lower and Middle Palaeolithic periods, datable to 200,000 to 50,000 years BCE or more but opinions are divided on the issue to include or not to include them in the category of Rock Art although their locations make them almost certain that these are not functional in everyday life, these are often located on the vertical sides of the rocks and are generally executed in groups. What magico-religious purpose they may have served is hardly possible to know at this stage of research. But certainly it was not done exclusively for self-satisfaction since these are found in Goa in India and in many other countries it had the potentiality of conveying messages to others visiting the places of their occurrence.

Lastly, how were these prehistoric painting traditions tied up with the classical traditions of Indian paintings, generally bracketed between 200 BCE and CE 1100, and later? Perhaps, not. There is no positive evidence for doing that. For example, the earliest Sātavāhana paintings of Ajantā of the second and first century BCE time-bracket were in no way inspired by the rock-shelter paintings. All the classical traditions were inspired by the organized religions – Buddhism, Jainism, Vaishnavism, Saivism, Sāktism, etc. and not by the Rock Art, although in some rock-shelters we do find them, as at some places in Gujarat, *stupa* is depicted but then it is more than clear that the former influenced the latter, and not the other way round.

OTHER FORMS OF STONE AGE ART AND ARCHITECTURE: EXPRESSIONS AND FORMS OF COMMUNICATION

The other forms of Rock Art done by engravings, peckings, etc. are very few in India. At Pañne, located near Ajantā, the excavations yielded engravings done on ostrich egg shells found embedded in the Upper Palaeolithic deposits. The rock engravings of the Neolithic period found in Andhra Pradesh, Goa and Karnataka generally include cattle and some wild animals.

Caves and rock-shelters are the natural abodes of men and gods although at times the Stone Age people erected stone wall by piling up stones of one kind or the other found in their vicinity. These walls served as protection devices against wind, rains and wild animals. The excavations conducted at Bhimbethkā rock-shelters have yielded the evidence of a few such structures.

Some kind of open-air shrines have been suspected in the Son Valley, in the Vindhyas, Mesolithic sites since heaps of stones, bearing naturally occurring parallel triangles, one within the other, due to water action, in the region of sandstone formations, were marked by the explorers. Since similar stones are still worshipped by the villagers living nearby, the explorers, J.D. Clarke and G.R. Sharma, felt that it could be the continuation of an old tradition – the triangles represent females in their mother goddess aspect.

Thus, in terms of Stone Age Art there is a lot of data-base but in terms of Stone Age Architecture in India, we have very limited evidence to work upon. In fact, bone and stone sculptures and engravings found in the Upper Palaeolithic deposits in Europe, have only rarely been found in Indian rock-shelter deposits. Only in deposits of the Billasurgam caves in Karnataka bone art works in engravings have been reported. Nevertheless, both are important components of methods doing something and communicating them to others. Shrines with stones having motifs created by nature certainly had magico-religious meaning underlying them which was shared by prehistoric community because the skill of communication was inherent in constructing even make-shift shrines.

CONCLUSIONS

Research on the communication systems of monkeys and apes through 1962 has been most ably summarized and interpreted by Marler. Most of the data represent work by field observers who were primarily interested in social structure, and the signals, and their meanings, used to implement and facilitate social interactions were more or less taken for granted. Only in the last year or so have communication systems themselves been the object of careful study and analysis. Marler has emphasized both the extraordinary complexity of the communication systems of primates and the heavy dependence of these systems on composite signals. Most frequently it is not a single signal that passes between two animals but a signal complex composed of auditory, visual, tactile, and, more rarely, olfactory signals.

Communication in some monkey species is based on a system of intergrading signals, whereas in others much more use is made of highly discrete signals. For example, most vervet sounds are of the discrete type, there being some 36 different sounds that are comparatively distinct both to the human ear and when analyzed by a sound spectrograph. In contrast, Rowell and Hinde have analyzed the sounds of the rhesus monkey and found that of 13 harsh noises, 9 belonged to a single intergrading subsystem expressing agonistic emotions.

As more and more study is done on primates it will probably be shown that their communication systems tend to be of mixed form in that both graded and discrete signals are used depending on the relative efficiency of one or the other form in serving a specific function. In concert this use of both discrete and intergrading signals and of composites from several sensory modes produces a rich potential for the expression of very slight but significant changes in the intensity and nature of mood in the signaling animal. Marler has emphasized that, except for calls warning of danger, the communication system is little applied to events outside the group. Communication systems in monkeys and apes are highly evolved in their capacity to express motivation of individuals and to facilitate social relationships. Without this ability to express mood, monkeys and apes would not be able to engage in the subtle and complicated social interactions that are a major feature of their adaptations.

As has been noted above, communication is basic to all creatures, including birds and mammals, but studies done so far in this respect are limited to primates and humans. Since all primates did not develop in human beings of today, the *Homo Sapiens Sapiens*, we can only surmise that what the Apes, nearest to humans, like chimpanzee do may have also been done by the Early man, called *Homo Erectus*, dated to around 1,00,000 years from now. Later on these methods of communication diversified and by 33,000 BCE Prehistoric humans in Europe developed the medium of Rock Art to communicate with other fellow beings – ideas, beliefs, hunting and gathering strategies, etc. eventually, by 4000 BCE the humans developed script to communicate through the languages which they had already evolved over three to four thousand years ago. This happened first in Mesopotamia (modern Iraq) followed by Egypt, India and China where between 3500 BCE and 2000 BCE we have archaeological remains to prove it.

BIBLIOGRAPHY

Chakravarty, K.K. and R.G. Bednarik, *Indian Rock Art and Global Context*, Rashtriya Manava Sangrahalaya, Bhopal, 2004

Gupta, S.P., *Elements of Indian Art* (Second Ed.), D.K. Printworld, New Delhi, 2006, pp. 1-8.

Washburn, S.L. and C. Jay Phyllis, (Eds.) *Perspectives on Human Evolution*, USA, 1968, pp. 206-207.

7

Communication in Pre-Modern India

Raghavendra Vajpeyi

Advances in science and technology have revolutionized the nature and scope of communication in today's world. The entire face of the earth comprising distant continents (including the frozen continent of Antarctica), separated from one another by a vast expanse of seas and oceans has become the defining feature of the evolving global village.

Aeroplanes and space vehicles can make one traverse the longest ever distances and satellite telephony and video-conferencing can make one have an almost immediate contact with people sitting in different countries and continents, as if all are seated across the table. Access to information and knowledge is just for the asking.

Traditional means of communication have been rendered outdated by mobile-cum-satellite telephony and email. Television can make one see on his TV set events actually happening, instead of waiting for the next day's newspapers.

But, things were not so before the dawn of the modern age. And that is what makes the present inquiry relevant in the context of nature and scope of communication in the Indian subcontinent in pre-modern times.*

The term modern will mean different time periods in different contexts. It began much earlier in Europe, but Indians experienced the dawn of modern age only after the East India Company gained its firm foot-hold in India, and it gradually introduced printing press, newspaper, railways, telephony, teleprinter, etc. received much needed direction and support under the patronage of the British Crown after the Indian uprising of 1857. Since then process of modernization has brought India *at par* with the rest of the world in the I.T. sector.

When we speak of pre-modern India, we propose to go back in time and begin our journey from the third millennium BC – the time she began shaping her cultural identity, and made her concrete responses to influences responsible for her distinctive cultural and civilizational mosaic.[1] Since then, a gradual unfolding of nature and scope of communication has continued in the Indian subcontinent.

Archaeology provides ample evidence on the success of third millennium BC Indians (i.e. Harappans) in conceiving, creating and effectively maintaining a network of transport and communication over the largest geo-political entity of the time.[2] Creation and maintenance of planned cities and satellite urban centres was the end product of the concept of reciprocity based relations between productive hinterland and manufacture-cum-trade centric urban centres. Harappans were successful in tapping raw-material zones existing within India and in other countries. They likewise exported their high value products and luxury items to lucrative markets existing in other countries.

Harappans had conceived the idea and concept of a multiracial, multilingual, multireligious and multicultural society. They also provided a common meeting ground to diverse cultural trends. But they had respect and goodwill for seemingly different socio-cultural moorings as the cornerstone of their composite society.[3] They were the real authors of the Indian concept of unity in diversity.

Harappans had conceived a unique method of integrating diverse ethnic, linguistic and cultural elements in their society. They provided them an unalterable position in a socio-ritual purity/impurity differential centric society. Birth in a particular class or group of privileged, less privileged or unprivileged section of society seems to have been accepted as an act of divine dispensation for peoples' own deeds in previous life. That is, it was a result of their own doing or undoing for which no one else could be held responsible. Birth in a privileged class was treated as the divine reward for good deeds and birth in servile class was, likewise, accepted as the divine retribution for bad deeds committed in previous birth. This hypothesis seems to be the only logical explanation for upsets or setbacks free unchanging socio-economic and political character of the mature Harappan society during its five century long existence.[4]

Archaeology provides us ample evidence on geometrically correct and true to measurement built houses, lanes, roads, right angle crossings in respect of Harappan town planning. Kiln-burnt bricks and pottery of different description and sizes, weights and measures (for weighing high value smallest items to semi precious to ordinary low value bulk items) indicate that Harappans had a sound knowledge of the concept of multiplication and division as arithmetical propositions. Their local, regional and long distance trade; monopoly on textile products, etc. religious beliefs-ranging from aniconic to theriomorphic to anthropomorphic divinities-their mythology and ritual practices, etc. offer clear evidence on the existence of oral and writing traditions among them.[5] The writing preserved on Harappan seals, etc. suggests that it had already passed the first two stages of its development and was a little short of reaching the alphabetic stage.[6]

The cultural content of the Harappan civilization was amply enriched by different religious rituals blended into one single unified stream of thought and communication of religious ideas and practices from generation to generation, such as, ritual bathing on a specific day, time and place (prototype of the latterday Kumbha bathing), normal bathing as a religious prerequisite of the worship of divinities; existence of a priestly class which conducted ceremonial worship etc., rituals and religious singing and temple dance performed by skilled female and male dancers.[7] The sacred bathing tradition seems to be at least five millennia old (if reference to the Great Bath of Mohenjodaro is given any credence.)[8] The tradition of sacred bathing finds largest number of people gathering at select places. Their devotion and religiosity heighten the serenity of the occasion.[9]

The five century long period of high urbanism of the Harappans suffered a catastrophic collapse because of the evil designs of nature and man alike. Drastic changes in climate, earthquakes, rise in river bed, floods, changes in the course of rivers, transformation of water channels and canals into mud lakes, etc. – were followed by epidemics of extraordinary proportions. Consequently, rural-urban communication and connectivity suffered a severe blow.[10]

The Harappan scientific temper and advanced technological know-how suffered a setback during the post Harappan period. No wonder, regression of civilization apparatus made the written word and writing tradition absolutely irrelevant. On the positive side, word of mouth and oral tradition received unprecedented boost. Entire religious and literary tradition of the early Aryans displayed a gigantic feat of memory, and the legacy of the *Ṛigvedic* text was systematically passed on by one generation of priestly class of scholars, teachers and students to next generation.[11]

Roughly a period of one thousand years had separated the bronze age Harappan civilization from the sixth century BC iron age urbanism. Logically speaking, the Harappan civilization too must have been the fruition of at least a thousand year long human endeavour. However, the second phase of urbanism was built upon a more solid foundation and, as such, it did not completely fade away during later phases of crises. Secondly, the second urbanization had virtually attained subcontinental character, thanks to the writing tradition that culminated in the evolution of the Brāhmī Script as a mode of communication throughout the length and breadth of the Indian sub-continent.[12]

The oral tradition remained the hallmark of brahmanical rural society. Writing tradition, on the other hand, received ready support from educated urban sections of society, especially rulers, administrators, traders, bankers and industry people.[13] Not only that, heterodox teachers, philosophers as well as intelligentsia specializing in various fields of material cultural and sciences welcomed reintroduction of the writing tradition and system. Buddhist and Jaina teachers accorded religious status to the writing system by associating it with the Creator (Brahmā) and called it Brāhmī.[14]

In the wake of the second urbanization both oral and writing traditions acquired the position of great means and systems of communication. Explorers, traders and religious missionaries frequented unknown and less known areas and regions of the Indian subcontinent.[15] Political adventurers/invaders followed the suit. Once new areas were conquered and annexed, effective steps were taken to retain and maintain administrative control over them. All the people who visited those areas made effective use of the word of mouth as means of communication.[16]

Sites and places, associated with mythological traditions acquired the status of religious centres or *tirthas*. They were periodically visited by followers of different religions. While some places were intimately connected with life and careers of great teachers, other places were accorded special status on the basis of other considerations.[17] Such centres were known for their religious buildings, monumental structures and religious art.[18] Religious art and architecture, sculptures and paintings became famous for their artistic sensibility. Sculptural relief panels of Bharhut and Sanchi documented the life of the Buddha in stone.[19] The Sarnath Buddha seated in *dharmachakra-pravartana mudrā*, depicting underneath the seat of the Lord the Wheel of Dhamma or righteousness and having deer on either side and his first five disciples [Sarnath Museum Catalogue No. 182 B] and the paintings in cave nos. 16 and 17 of Ajanta are finest examples of religious art in perpetual communication with the visitors.[20]

It is debatable whether man's first rhythmic musical intonation and expression was the result of intensity of his love for his beloved or was it the product of intensity of his devotion for his personal deity. But, repetitive religiosity and ritualistic functioning of temple music and dance seem to have become the second most significant aspect of music and dance. Thus, religion brought practitioners of religious music and devotees in perpetual communion with each other.[21]

The same sublime and ecstatic partnership was developed by sufi saints and their disciples during their intensely religious dances called *samaa*.[22] Music and songs of medieval saints attracted ordinary folks and elite alike, and had great mass appeal. Music became a great means of communication of social message and also a harbinger of change and reformation in medieval India.[23]

We have a strong feeling that secular arts and music were product of much more advanced and sophisticated society. Emotions, sentiments, language, diction, rhythm and tune all put together – contributed to integration and blending of creator with his creation to such a level that the audience became spell bound and forgetful of its own physical surroundings and material reality. In that case also, sense of rhythm and manifestation of emotions elevated people to such a spiritual plane where words lost their relevance.

No doubt, verbal communication ranging from private conversation to debate and discussion to sermons and teachings of saintly people had much greater impact than written communication. But, when the same message or information was passed on by a second or third source, chances of misunderstanding based misinformation or misleading information were equally great. Variations of language zones and occasional speech defect/defects of secondary communicator could also multiply problems of communication.

Such a situation normally does not exist in the case of written communication. Not only that, a document can reach its farthest destination in its original form. Educated and literate people can themselves read it. Illiterate messenger does not hamper its reachability to its destination. Until half a century back, post offices and postmen often acted as a powerful communication bridge between unlettered senders of letters etc. and their equally unlettered family member recipients of their letters. The same type of communication channel must have existed in ancient and medieval past. Illiterate class of rural and urban masses must have been informed about administrative decisions in that manner in the past. Lower bureaucracy seems to have had been charged with that duty, and also with that of reporting back different shades of public opinion to the concerned authority. The same bureaucratic channel must have kept the relevant authority informed about natural and manmade calamities and crises. So also, it would have informed the masses about relief measures being initiated.[24] Occasions of rulers' religious liberality like grant of cash money and landed property, etc. to religious establishments belonging to their own faith as well as to other faiths enhanced their popularity quotient.[25]

If communication channel between the rulers and the ruled became clogged, either because of inefficiency of bureaucracy or because of its apathy or its conspiratorial attitude against the ruling sovereign, state tended to collapse from within. This is what had happened in the case of collapse of the Mauryan empire.[26] Muhammand-bin-Tughluq, the greatest scholar and forward looking Sultan of the fourteenth century Delhi, was also a victim of such circumstances.[27]

Mauryan emperor Aśoka was the greatest communicator known to pre-modern India.[28] He prepared the blue-print of an absolutely new, and till then unthought of, war-free and peace centric New World Order.[29] What he communicated to the world and his own people through his edits in the third century BC India, the world came to realize its relevance and necessity only after the tragic experience of two World Wars.[30]

What made Aśoka one of the greatest human beings in world history was his realization of the futility of war as long term solution for outstanding political problems between two sovereign states.[31] He unilaterally decided to put an end to the policy of war, and to divert the saved resources on measures aimed at offering a permanent solution of problems faced by his contemporary world. He spent fabulous amounts of state resources on his World Health Scheme aimed at providing medical facilities for the treatment of man and animal alike across all natural and man made borders of his time.[32] So also, he sent his messengers and missionaries for moral uplifting of man – emphasizing significance of compassion, love, kindness and happiness for all and sundry-all aimed at making the world a better and dignified home for all the living beings.[33] That was a marvellous way of his communicating and transmitting some of India's eternal values to other centres of civilization in his time as far as Egypt and Greece, let alone the far corners of South and South East Asia.[34]

Aśoka decided to begin his humanistic activities at the grassroot level from his own subcontinental empire.[35] He knew it well that political inheritance had allowed him the right to preside over the destiny of his subjects, but his social consciousness made him feel responsible for the well-being of all the people in his contemporary world.[36] He also tried to ensure existence of a high moral value system as the regulatory mechanism of all social, economic, political, religious, linguistic and ethnic relationships in his contemporary pluralistic Indian society.[37]

Decipherable and intelligible writing system was introduced in India in the wake of the iron-age urbanism of the sixth century BC.[38] Like other technology supported material sciences and activities, it too had matured within a period of the following couple of centuries. It is a debatable issue whether Indians had inherited and improved upon the writing system bequeathed by the Harappans or that the Aryans had introduced their own writing system. Or else they had borrowed and adopted the writing system from the West Asian Aramaic traders and other people who had been frequenting the Indian borderlands. Champions of each theory have existed in India and elsewhere.[39]

One thing is, however, very clear. The Brāhmī script of Aśoka's inscriptions happened to be clear, bold and systematic and capable of accommodating new sound values and characters denoting them. That quality made it mother of all latterday north Indian scripts. Although it had a definite relationship with the Magadhan Prakrit language, it was not disadvantaged in the case of other Prakrits then in vogue in areas and regions away from the central zone of the empire. Aśoka allowed use of the Kharoshṭhī script in the north-western frontier region as a measure of communication with the people there, but he insisted upon use of the official language Prakrit throughout the Indian mainland of his empire.[40] However, he did not suffer from linguistic or scriptal bigotry. He knew that West Asian trading community had its settlements in Kabul and Kandhar cities in the Afghanistan portion of his empire. Kandhar was a more cosmopolitan city and it also had a Greek colony. Therefore, Aśoka decided to send his message of Dhamma to the West Asian and Greek traders and settlers there in their respective languages and scripts (i.e., in Aramaic language and script and in Greek language and script.)[41] That is, he knew that the language and script of a people were valuable means and tool of communication and he used them effectively and widely.

Last days of the Mauryan empire found the Indo-Greek branch of the Bactrian Greeks in possession of the Lahore and Sialkot areas of the present-day Pakistan. Although they had been using the Greek language and script on their coins, nothing else of significance has been found in those areas.[42] The Parthians, Sassanids, Scythians and Kushāṇas established their kingdoms in succession. Although their linguistic traditions manners and customs had their impact on Indian society and culture, they did not much influence the Indian script tradition.[43] Kharoshṭhī script was in vogue in Mathura region and in the north-west zone.[44] Prakrits of the regional variety were used in western India and the Deccan. Later on, they contributed to various stages of transformation of Prakrit into semi-Sanskritised Prakrit to Prakritised Sanskrit.[45] Finally standardized and literary Sanskrit came to be used by the time of Śaka Mahākshatrapa Rudradaman I who used it in his Junagarh Rock Inscription of the Śaka year 72 (=AD 150.)[46] Elsewhere, Prakrits continued to survive till as late as the fourth century. The imperial Guptas adopted Sanskrit as their official language. Political successors of the Guptas in north India and the Deccan continued to use Sanskrit as their official language till the end of the seventh century.[47] By the ninth century, regional states switched over to their regional languages and contributed to the evolution of regional scripts and regional personality.[48] They adversely affected north-south connectivity, earlier established by Prakrit and Sanskrit languages and Brāhmī script. Tamil language and script reached its high watermark in the time of great Choḷa conquerors-Rājarāja and Rājendra Choḷa.[49] However, Sanskrit, continued to remain the language for academic and scholarly pursuits in north and south India alike.[50]

Although the Gupta state and government had been the product of classico-feudal economy and polity,[51] the dawn of regional dynasties manifested onward march of feudalism in the early medieval period. Eighth to tenth century period witnessed unsettled condition in north India as a result of triangular warfare among the Gurjara-Pratihāras, Pālas and Rāshṭrakūṭas.[52] Arabs took full advantage of peoples' dissatisfaction in Sindh against their reigning king Dahir. They invaded Sindh and Multan and conquered it in the second decade of the eighth century and made Arabic as their official language and script.[53] Although Arabic remained the language of Islam and its sacred works, the eleventh and twelfth century Turkish conquerors and rulers established their sultanate in north India in the first decade of the thirteenth century and introduced Persian as their official language and script.[54]

Sultans of Delhi and their nobility had to depend heavily on the support of their Indian Muslim camp followers who constituted majority in the army of the sultanate. They were the people who gave birth to a mixed Indo-Persian language having good number of north Indian words and phrases. That language was spoken in military cantonment markets (Urdu Bazaar). Because of its that origin it was called Urdu. Its more systematized and standardized counterpart language was known as Hindwi – the prototype of the latterday Hindi language.[55]

European traders like Portuguese, British, French and Dutch enriched the Indian linguistic horizon. In the 19th century, English language displaced Persian from its position of official language. Long period of the use of English in India has virtually accorded it the status of an Indian language.[56]

Since the time of the Mauryan empire, the knowledge of official language and script paved the way for connectivity of administrative headquarters with distant areas of the state. Provincial governors and their counsellors and bureaucracy had been supposed to be fairly acquainted with people, language and problems, etc. of their administrative zone.[57] Bureaucracy acted as an effective bridge between rulers and the ruled. Traders and religious missionaries constituted yet another group of bilingual and multilingual people. They made no small contribution to keeping of communication channels open. Scholars born in different language zones also produced their scholarly writings in time honoured languages of repute, like Prakrit, Sanskrit, Persian, Hindi and Urdu-cutting across all linguistic, religious and cultural barriers.[58] Knowledge of contemporary international languages like Aramaic, Greek, Arabic, Persian etc. contributed to greater connectivity with the rest of the world.[59] Bilingual interpreters were known to have existed in India and elsewhere since the dawn of its earliest civilization.[60]

Oral means of communication enjoyed great antiquity and remained most authentic and personalized means of communication. From ancient and medieval times down to the present, written documents are usually supported by verbal communication-ranging from diplomats' visit, lectures, seminars, discussions, conferences and parliamentary proceedings, etc. But the communication channel is occasionally impaired when the message is passed on by/to the third party, mostly because of the inability of the communicator to reproduce it correctly verbatim.

Written language and its documents donot suffer from such drawback. They can travel the longest distance without any possibility of being altered or corrupted. So also, the possibility of correction of draft has always existed upto its final rendition. Even at final stage, if any word is found forgotten or wrongly written that too can be incorporated/corrected.[61] However, in early medieval times when tradition of copying of manuscripts was introduced, some copyists familiar with the language but not with the subject matter, at times, made unwarranted corrections.[62]

We can close our statement on communication in pre-modern India by underlining the following points:

(a) Oral communication channel became meaningful right from the time modern man (homo sapiens sapiens) could utter his first meaningful words.[63] From that point of view, tradition of written communication happens to be yesterday's development;[64]

(b) Language and script complement each other. Where neither of them is known, we remain as clueless as in the case of the Harappan writing;[65]

(c) Man's desire to make his records timeless has contributed to the beginning of the era of engraved writing on stone and other materials;[66]

(d) Decipherable writing tradition encouraged scholars to prepare manuscript copies of works belonging to both secular and religious categories. Skilled calligraphers[67] were encouraged by rulers such as Mughals to prepare manuscript copies of the holy Quran and gems of Persian literature, including biographies of rulers;[68] and

(e) At least from the time of the Mauryan Empire, effective communication channels were operational in the Indian subcontinent. Horse happened to be the fastest moving animal in service of man. Horse rider carriers (*sāḍinī sawār*) of post and documents travelled long distances. Medieval Indian ruler Sher Shah deserves the credit for having successfully reduced the time distance factor, by inventing the relay dak system (postal service) for sending and receipt of information, administrative documents, royal commands and orders from one end of the empire to another end. It caused lesser strain on horse-rider messenger and had added advantage of relatively faster speed.[69]

But all this would appear primitive to information technology savvy young man of tomorrow's India.

NOTES AND REFERENCES

* Mohan Sundara Rajan, *The Telecom Story*, Delhi, 1996, pp. 1-87.

1. Bridget and Raymond Allchin, *The Rise of Civilization in India and Pakistan*, Cambridge, 1996; Delhi, 1999, pp. 131 &ff., 167-71, 192-95
2. Ibid., p. 25.
3. Ibid., pp. 131 & ff, 167-71, 192-95.
4. Ibid., p. 217, Harappa R-37 cemetery had skeletal remains of four racial types. Harappa H cemetery indicated arrival of new people.
5. Ibid., pp. 171-83, 185-87, 213-17.

6. Ibid., pp. 212-13.
7. Ibid., pp. 180-81, 205.
8. Ibid., p. 180.
9. Gavin Flood, *An Introduction to Hinduism,* Cambridge, 1996, pp. 15, 104, 109, 143, 192, 212-14; *A Cultural History of India* (ed.) A.L. Basham, Oxford, 1975, Delhi, 1984, pp. 237-38, 287, 194-95.
10. *The History and Culture of the Indian* People, Vol. 1, *The Vedic Age,* (eds.) R.C. Majumdar, A.D. Pusalkar, London, 1951, p. 249.
11. *Ṛigveda,* vii. 103.
12. It will be logical to believe that settlement formation in rural areas must have needed sufficient time to reach the stage of self-sufficiency, followed by that of their surplus generation capacity. So also, possibility of surplus transfer to urban areas, and consequential rural-urban interdependence would have preceded the dawn of the Mature Harappan phase (circa 2250-1750 BC ± 150 years).
13. V. Gordon Childe, "The Urban Revolution", *The Town Planning Journal,* Liverpoole, XXI, 1 April, 1950 pp. 3-17 (cited in A. Ghosh, *The city in Early Historical India,* Simla, 1973, p. 23 & ff.); R.S. Sharma, *Perspectives in Social and Economic History of Ancient India,* Delhi, 1983, 1995, pp. 162-67.
14. G.S. Gai, *Introduction to Indian Epigraphy,* Mysore, 1986, pp. 14-15; T.P. Verma, *The Palaeography of Brāhmī Script,* Varanasi 1971, pp. 4-7.
15. Tradition avers that Agastya was the first north Indian to have crossed the *Vindhyas;* Vijaya *Siṁha* colonized erstwhile Ceylon, presently known as Sri Lanka, anciently called *Siṁhala;* and Kauṇḍinya and Kambu-Svāyambhuva were the two Indian leaders who contributed to colonization of ancient Combodia.
16. Mahāpadma Nanda to Alauddin Khilji to Aurangzeb – all sent their invading armies across the Vindhyas; and after conquest and annexation of conquered territory, bureaucratic arrangements were made for their administration. Communication with the regional and local people was possible either through interpreters or by bureaucracy equipped with skill and proficiency in regional languages – but mostly by word of mouth.
17. R.S. Sharma, *Urban Decay in India,* Delhi, 1987, pp. 108-21, 178-85.
18. *The History and Culture of the Indian People,* Vol. 11, *The Age of Imperial Unity,* (eds.) R.C. Majumdar, A.D. Pusalkar, Bombay, 1990, pp. 483-580; *The History and Culture of the Indian People,* Vol. III, *The Classical Age,* (eds.) R.C. Majumdar, A.D. Pusalkar, Bombay, 1953, 1962, pp. 471-553.
19. The Bharhut Buddhist panels have been supported by captions engraved underneath, though the Sanchi panels are devoid of those captions. Ibid, pp. 510-15.

20. *Sarnath Museum Catalogue No. 182-B* and the Ajanta Cave Nos. 16 and 17 have the universe of Buddhism vividly depicted in the frescoes – which also flourished in the Gupta-Vākāṭaka age see, also, *The Çlassical Age*, pp. 523-25, 547-50.
21. Allchin, op.cit., pp. 180, 203-05.
22. A.L. Srivastava, *Medieval Indian Culture,* Agra, 1975, pp. 65-68.
23. Ibid., Flood, op.cit., p.98, Basham, op.cit., pp. 253-54, 469.
24. *Select Inscriptions,* D.C. Sircar, Calcutta, 1965, pp. 18-19 Aśoka's Rock Edict III, ll. 1-3, 6, Rock Edict VI, ll. 1-24, pp. 24-25.
25. A.C. Arora, *Bhartiya Itihas ka Mughal tatha British Kal,* Jalandhar, 1985, pp. 79-147.
26. H.C. Raychaudhuri, *Political History of Ancient India,* Calcutta, 1953, pp. 353, 364-71.
27. A.B. Pandey, *Early Medieval India,* Allahabad, 1960, 1993, pp. 199-202.
28. After his twelfth coronation year, Aśoka had inaugurated his scheme of informing his subjects about almost everything that he thought was desirable and could be universally practised; and what he considered bad and undesirable and was to be given up. In order to inform and educate his subjects, he issued his rock, pillar and cave inscriptions between his coronation year 12-27 which covered almost all the nodal points of his empire.
29. Sircar, op.cit., pp. 20-21, 34-35 (Aśoka's Rock Edict IV, XIII).
30. Ferdinand Schevill, *A History of Europe,* London, 1947, pp. 750 ff & 887-89.
31. Sircar, op.cit, p.20 (Rock Edict IV- bherī ghoso aho Dhamma ghoso).
32. Aśoka's Rock Edicts II & XIII.
33. Ibid.
34. Rock Edict II, 1-8.
35. Ibid.
36. Ibid.
37. II to XIII.
38. Pāṇini, *Ashṭādhyāyī,* 3.2.27 "lipi-dipi yavanānī;" G.S. Gai, *Introduction to Indian Epigraphy,* Mysore, 1986, 14-15; T.P. Verma, *The Palaeography of Brāhmī Script in North India,* Varanasi, 1971, pp. 4-7; R.S. Sharma, op.cit., pp. 108, 21, 178-85.
39. Gai, op.cit., pp.12-16; D.C. Sircar, *Numismatic and Epigraphical Studies,* Calcutta, 1977, pp. 85, 253; *Indian Antiquary,* vol. XXXIII, pp. 15, 253; A.H. Dani, *Indian Palaeography,* Delhi, 1986, pp. 22,28; David Diringer, *Writing,* London, 1962, pp. 144-55, I.J. Gelb, *A Study of Writing,* 1969, p. 22.
40. Gai, op.cit.; Sircar, *Numismatic and Epigraphical Studies,* p.85; Except Kharoshṭhī inscriptions engraved at Shahbazgarhi and Mansehra in Pakistan – Afghanistan border area, his all other inscriptions in the Indian subcontinent were in Brāhmī script.

41. However, Aśoka's Pul-i-Duranta (Kabul) and Sher-i-Kuna (Kandhar) inscriptions were addressed to the Aramaic speaking West Asian traders etc. settled there and, as such, were in the Aramaic language and script. Since a Greek colony was also flourishing at Kandhar, another minor rock edict was engraved there in the Greek language and script.
42. Raychauduri, op.cit., pp. 378-89.
43. Ibid., pp. 425 & ff.
44. Sircar, *Numismatic and Epigraphical* studies, p. 85.
45. Sircar, *Select Inscriptions*, pp. 164-175.
46. Ibid., pp. 175-80.
47. *The Classical Age*, pp. 245-46.
48. Ibid., vol IV, *The Age of Imperial Kanauj* (eds.) R.C. Majumdar, A.D. Pusalkar, Bombay, 1993, pp. 11, 35, 38.
49. Ibid., vol V, *The Struggle for Empire*, (eds.) R.C. Majumdar, A.D. Pusalkar, A.K. Majumdar, Bombay, 1989, pp. 234 & ff.
50. Ibid., vol V, *The Struggle for Empire*, (eds.) R.C. Majumdar, A.D. Pusalkar, A.K. Majumdar, Bombay, 1989, pp. 234 &
51. Raghavendra Vajpeyi, "Gupta Perception of Indian Reality and Feudalism," *Proceeding of the Indian History Congress*, 1987, Goa, pp. 95-102.
52. *The Classical Age*, pp. 245-46.
53. *The Age of Imperial Kanauj*, p.198 & ff.
54. *A Comprehensive History of India*, vol. III, pt 1, (eds.) R.C. Majumdar, K.K. Dasgupta, Delhi, 1981, p. 436 & ff.
55. Srivastava, op.cit., pp. 78-79, 94, 112-13, Arora, op.cit., pp. 452-53 & ff.
56. Basham, op.cit., p. 406.
57. Raychaudhuri, op.cit., pp. 271-94, 307-21.
58. The sixth century BC heterodox teachers Mahāvīra and Buddha had addressed their followers in people's languages Prakrit and Pali and Jaina and Buddhist literature adhered to the same principle. Although the Mahāyāna Buddhism switched over to Sanskrit language, the fifth century Valabhī conference of the jainas preferred to stick to the Prakrit language. The south Indian poet Bhāravi wrote his epic *Kirātārjunīya* in Sanskrit under the patronage of the Pallavas of Kāñchi. The great brāhmaṇa reformer of Hinduism from Kalady (Kerala), Ādi Śaṅkarāchārya effectively used Sanskrit language for his writings and discourses. The Jaina author Somadeva Sūri wrote his polity book *Nītivākyāmṛita* in Sanskrit. Even during the high noon of Choḷa imperialism, Tamil inscriptions continued to have historical introduction in Sanskrit language in them. In medieval period Amir Khusro was an outstanding scholar of Persian and Sanskrit who immensely contributed to growth and standardization

of Hindwi language and literature. Likewise, Mulla Wajhi made valuable contribution to Dakkhini Hindi literature. Sher Shah made Hindi paṭṭā (revenue record) copy of state demand note Qabūliyat written in Persian language and script to be given to peasantry as an effective means of contact and communication with his subjects at grassroot level. His contemporary Hindi poet and Sufi scholar Malik Muhammad Jayasi wrote his epic *Padmāvata* in Hindi language and Persian script. Prince Salim's (Jahangir) tutor and high ranking Mughal noble Abur Rahim Khan-i-Khana was an eminent scholar of Persian, Sanskrit and Hindi languages as well as an outstanding astrologer. He wrote poems in Hindi and was also a contemporary of Tulsidas. Mirza Raja Jai Singh and Guru Gobind Singh were among the leading lights of the 17th century literary style of Persian language. Although Shivaji was among the people who did not much like reading and writing, he too had availed fair knowledge of Islam and its tenets. The leading light of Bengal renaissance Raja Ram Mohan Roy was also a scholar of Persian and editor of a Persian newspaper.

61. A classical example of such uncalled for correction is the case of south Indian Jain scholar Mallinātha's correction "Siṅdhu" for "Vaṅkshu" name of the Hūṇa river mentioned by Kālidāsa in his *Raghuvamsa,* iv.67. The 12th century Kashmiri commentator of *Raghuvamsa,* Vallabha has shown that Mallinatha was wrong, see, for details, K.B. Pathak, "Kālidāsa and the Hūṇas of the Oxus Valley", *Indian Antiquary,* vol. XLI, 1914. p. 266.
62. *Introduction to Indian Epigraphy,* pp. 3-4.
63. Ibid, Homo sapiens sapiens had emerged sometime in or about one million years before now, but writing system could not find any shape before third millennium BC.
64. Allchin, op.cit., pp. 212-12.
65. Aśoka's Pillar Edict VI, ll. 21-22.
66. Arora, op.cit., pp. 74-75.
67. Basham, op.cit, 312.
68. Srivastava, op.cit., pp. 78-79, 94, 112-13, Arora, op.cit., pp. 452-53 & ff.
69. Srivastava, op.cit., pp. 78-79, 94, 112-13, Arora, op.cit., pp. 452-53 & ff.

8

Satellite in Education: Edusat in the Teacher Training and Education

Rajendra Mishra

INTRODUCTION

The first published idea on satellite broadcast came from an American writer of Science Fact and Fiction Prof. Arthur C. Clarke in his article "Wireless World" in 1945. Clarke foresaw that it would be possible to provide complete radio coverage of the world from just 3 satellites, provided they are precisely placed in a particular path known as 'Geostationary orbit'.

The first artificial satellite into the orbit was put by the Russians on 4th October, 1957 and that time onwards techniques to put machinery and men into space have rapidly advanced.

The first communication satellite capability of relaying messages immediately was launched in 1962 called Tilstar, which circulated the earth at a height between 960 km and 5600 km orbit also known as highly electrical. This enabled it to connect ground station in the USA and UK for only about half an hour each day. This was entirely funded by private sources and represented a significant steps towards the commercialization of the global satellite communication network.

The first commercial satellite known as Intelsat-I, called Early Bird, was launched on 6th April, 1965. It weighed under 40 kg in orbit and offered 240 television circuits or 1 TV channel. This marked Intelsat Early Bird as the world's first commercial communication satellite for television, voice and facsimile.

In India, the first satellite communication was conducted in the year 1975-76 with ATS-6 loaned by USA to the Government of India for one year to use satellite in transmitting TV programmes to remote villages in the region. With the launch of INSAT satellite in the early 80s, India started using satellite communication for its own developmental purposes as well as for education from its indigenous based satellite system known as INSAT. Today India has reached almost all corners of the country as well as other parts of the world, wherever INSAT satellite signals are being received. Today India has several INSAT satellites in the orbit and currently INSAT 4-A has been put into the orbit and other satellite are also in pipeline.

It was the vision of Dr. Vikram Sarabhai to use satellite broadcasting to reach those who needed it most, e.g. rural masses. He had visualized this as a system for social transformation, as no other method had the possibility of reaching out to the most backward region so quickly by providing the information in the most understandable manner.

The SITE experiment which is known as Satellite Instructional Television Experiment gave vision of using satellite for social transformation that hired many experts from the field of engineering, science, communication, managers as well as social scientists.

Educational institutions of the country have continuously endeavoured to use the latest technologies to support the process of education. For this purpose we need a system which can sustain the increasing demand. The challenge of the present world is to stay updated every moment with the changing world. It was the vision of Prof. Satish Dhawan, former Chairman, ISRO, who started discussion on development of satellite exclusively for educational purposes. To support his challenge and vision ISRO launched EDUSAT, a satellite, exclusively dedicated to education on September 20, 2004 with the major objectives to provide support to both formal and non-formal education system in India through low cost ground system.

ABOUT EDUSAT

EDUSAT provides an extended 'C' band national beam, a KU band national beam and 5 KU band regional beams. The regional beams will facilitate in imparting education in the regional languages. The access to education among different segments of our population is quite uneven. As there are several challenges for planners and administrators of education in India, it was felt essential to utilize the system which can fill this gap by way of utilizing communication technology with quantity at across generous cost community, rural urban and geographical areas. The EDUSAT provides communication capacities to meet the requirements of different sectors of education. Be it primary, secondary, tertiary/higher, professional or be it class or distance learning. As per the document by DECU/ISRO, EDUSAT strengthens educational efforts, by augmenting curriculum based teaching, providing effective teacher trainer, community participation, increasing access to education and access to new technologies through an effective ground segment configuration.

Objectives of EDUSAT

(1) Acquiring experts in the setting up and operation of education oriented multimedia, multicasting and interactive network to support teaching and learning activity;
(2) Evaluate the effectiveness of such interactive network for learning and education;
(3) Train the user agencies to understand the organizational, managerial, technical and software requirements to run an interactive network on an operational basis;
(4) Experiment with different presentation genres and formats using interactive multimedia multicasting;
(5) Involve and encourage different users and subject experts in the production of educational software;
(6) To create a response – sensitive organizational and management structure to enable mid course correction and create sustainable system;
(7) Evolve modular network architecture to cater to different sectors of education as well as different regions; and,
(8) Adoption of these modules by different agencies in the country in operational phase.

The use of EDUSAT has been planned in 3 phases:

In Phase-I known as Pilot Phase, before the launch of EDUSAT and to continue thereafter also a few selected institutions were taken for networking through INSAT 3B. The basic objectives were to explore the feasibility of IT networking for synchronous learning, for video streaming concept at a very low data ready for "video conferencing quality", to arrive at a feasible practical solution of a network cooperation, research for cost reduction through indigenous network in similar size network and finally to address the issues of synchronous learning to interested community by highlighting the requirement of content generation, multimedia media foundation and development of resources. Phase-I was started in January, 2004 as a part of satellite communication activity of SAC DECU/ISRO.

The Pilot Phase was initially commenced using INSAT 3A KU band transponder for distance learning programme of 3 universities in Maharashtra, Karnataka and Madhya Pradesh.

All the 3 user agencies attracted the groups of students, teachers and trainers at varied levels through this Pilot Phase. One multimedia distance education network in Pilot Phase stage include a hub, 50 SITs and 50 Non-interactive receive only terminals for classroom functioning.

Phase-II – In this phase which is semi-operational, it was planned to establish national and regional EDUSAT network. At the national level, digital video broadcasting regional level satellite has been introduced as centralized signal network for the whole nation. DVB-RCS technology allows multicasting wireless access, two way satellite communication with permanent connectivity and allocation of bandwidth on demand. It is an open standard and not priority. This facility can be used with one sub-hub and having about 100-200 classroom per user agency (see diagram 1). Apart from the interactive terminals it is also proposed to set up searchable educational material archives.

Phase-III – In this phase which is already on ISRO, it will provide 3 satellite time station hub and few SITs. All the other SITs and ROTs have to be financed by user agencies. With this objective in mind, ISRO has already distributed the national beam to the 5 user agencies for making use of it by way of utilizing the same for the purpose of delivery of lectures from one centralized classroom to various locations through dedicated system. These user agencies are UGC-CEC for higher education, IGNOU for distance education, NCERT for school education, AICTE for technical education, etc. All the above agencies are trying to use the satellite as per the objectives mentioned above and per the objectives of their institutions. In the following paras the author is going to discuss the role of UGC-CEC as utilization of EDUSAT network for

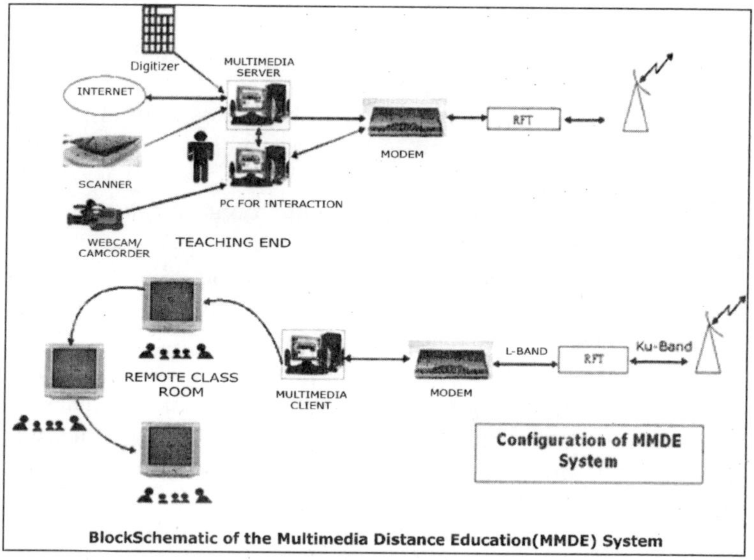

Diagram 1.

delivering lectures on different specialized subject areas, imparting training to the teachers, multimedia staff, using network for interactivity for the above purpose, skill development transfer to the remote areas sitting in Delhi and also for delivering various courses through EDUSAT network through interactive mode and the use of network for video on demand.

UTILIZATION OF UGC-CEC NATIONAL BEAM

At present UGC-CEC is having 58 SITs all over the country. These SITs are distributed in the institutions covering 17 EM^{2}RCs, 12 ASCs, 9 universities/colleges of potential excellence and 19 universities/colleges in remote areas including women's universities. This network is already expanded in the North East, where CEC is going to put 80 ROTs as well as 4 new SITs for the purpose of development of educational communication in the universities/colleges of North East States.

PHILOSOPHY

The Philosophy and moto of CEC is to reach out to the unreachable, providing quality higher education by empowering people with the power of knowledge and skills. As per Prof. G.D. Sharma, Director, CEC,

> we wish to package the knowledge, disseminate the quality knowledge under countrywide virtual classroom in different subjects and make the expertise of eminent teachers available to all, provide opportunities to teachers and students for synchronous and asynchronous interaction to solve their problems and help them acquiring quality knowledge in their desired areas of study.

APPROACH

The approach of CEC is to involve universities/colleges teachers, EM^2RCs, ASCs, other eminent scholars/teachers in packaging the knowledge in different subjects with the use of multimedia inputs and to provide all the networked institutions to act as classroom and teaching ends for selected subject areas or the areas of their specialization. Others means/institutions having classroom will also have an opportunity to act as teaching end in the selected areas.

METHODOLOGY

CEC provides opportunities to all the teachers, media professionals working in EM^2RCs and teachers' trainers in the ASCs in transferring skill to develop e-content material including the basic knowledge of instructional design methodology for development of subject material for the purpose of e-content, as well as development of syllabus based topics in the form of lectures which can be used for telecast in the 24 hour higher education channel. By this method CEC is training the teachers located in various parts of the country to develop their own skills for making teaching and learning more interesting with the use of multimedia inputs. The use of graphics, animation and special effects as well as other instructional design methods to impart the knowledge makes teaching and learning more absorbing and interesting.

CEC is using EDUSAT network for these trainings in the following manner:

Initially, CEC asks for nomination of teachers, multimedia personnel from universities/colleges as well as from EM^2RCs of

UGC-CEC for the purpose of giving 21 days training as a capacity building programme for multimedia e-content development. After selecting these teachers, CEC provides them with all facilities like boarding and lodging including TA/DA and gives training in multimedia lab at Delhi for 21 days. With the availability of EDUSAT network, CEC also encourages other institutions located in various parts of the country, where multimedia loaded software PCs are available to impart the same capacity building skill transfer using live demonstration of lectures and practical sessions from Delhi studio. In this approach, CEC organizes lecture-cum-demonstration by the subject experts in different areas of skill transfer in the morning session, and in the afternoon, practical sessions are organized. The experts give training to the trainee teachers sitting in various parts of the country, wherever they have been registered for this purpose to get guided and do the practicals sitting in their own locations with the help of instructions received from Delhi Live. In this process they can also immediately clarify their doubts related to their difficulties with the teachers/instructors sitting at Delhi and also demonstrate the same through live mode to overcome the same. With the use of distance network, it has become much easier to train more number of teachers at any given time without much constraints. This also has increased the capacity of training programmes to a large extent where similar facilities are available at various institutions wherever SITs are located.

Till now CEC has conducted 5 such training programmes in which teachers sitting at Baramula, Srinagar, Patiala, Mysore, Pune, Coimbatore and Ahmedabad have been trained through this method and they have at the end of the training delivered deliverables as per the requirement of the training in the form of e-content modules and short learning objects for completion of their training course.

EDUSAT gives flexibility to the teacher trainees and others to use the information, communication and technology in a much effective and lucid way to impart knowledge skills as well as make the teaching and learning more interesting with the technology enabled learning. Although presently EDUSAT has its own limitation, I am sure with the improvement in the system EDUSAT can be used very well for asynchronous and synchronous learning anytime anywhere with the help of web cast. This can also be used for solving the problem of clarifying doubts by students from various parts of the country directly with the best teachers through the live mode.

USES OF EDUSAT FOR TEACHERS

With the availability of EDUSAT network, a lecturer/teacher/ subject expert/presenter can utilize the system by way of using multimedia presentation to make his/her presentation more lucid and interesting. Through EDUSAT mode while delivering the lecture, one cannot only make the power point presentation but can also use video, audio, graphics and animation with the multimedia inputs to make the presentation more live and make understanding easier with the use of good visuals, daily live examples as well as graphics and animations which demonstrate the action and reaction in the classroom situation itself. EDUSAT is a boon for both teachers and learners by way of getting good information or knowledge through live interactions with each other. In addition one can utilize this facility for downloading the material available for subject related areas and specially live lectures through video on demand basis.

LIMITATIONS OF EDUSAT

As the Satellite is mainly using KU Band and Extended C Band, the signals could be only received through either KU Band dishes known as SITs or through dedicated dish antennas for the reception of the signals. The signals can also be received through Receive only Terminals (ROTs) but interactivity cannot be done for return path. Another limitation is the availability of bandwidth on return path for more than one user. ISRO needs to look into these shortcomings of EDUSAT to improve VLC path for better interactivity which is the very basic objective of EDUSAT Network. It is also required to create a user manual to help the respective institutions, giving details of all the equipments to be installed in the form of computers, cameras and studio setups for the purpose of classroom teaching and interactivity including software and hardware required. This will help the users to understand the basic requirements with standard specifications to make the connectivity effective as well as will give edge to the users.

CONCLUSION

To conclude one can say that opportunities are enormous. With the concerted efforts of technology enabled learning we can overcome the limitations of space, time and also manpower up to a large extent. This would not only enable the teachers to update and reach the students at large but also enable the students as well as the masses to reach the best teachers available in the country. EDUSAT is a boon for educational fraternity. It is an opportunity to make teaching learning more interesting by way of having live interaction for imparting skill or building capacity sitting in various locations with the help of technology enabled learning without the constraint of distance and bigger infrastructure.

REFERENCES

1. Arthur C. Clarke, *Extra Relays: Wireless World*, October 1945.
2. O.P. Khushu, *Satellite Communication in Asia: An Overview*, Media Asia, Volume 20 No. 1., 1993.
3. Arvind Sinha, K. M. Parmar, *INSAT Affects Study – Television and Rural Life: A Closer Look*, Technical Report, ISRO, January, 1995.
4. Hansa Joshi, Javed & Hashmi, *Research Guide Book for EDUSAT Utilization*, DECO/ISRO, Ahmedabad, December, 2005.
5. G.D. Sharma, *Reaching out to all with Quality Higher Education: The Philosophy, Approach and Methodology towards the use of EDUSAT Network in Higher Education*, CEC Television News, December 2005.

(The opinion expressed in this paper is of the author and may not necessarily be in agreement with the policy of the organization in which he is working.)

9

Emergence of Radio and Television As Instruments of Mass Communication on Development and Social Change (With Particular Reference to India)

Sunil Misra

BRIEF BACKGROUND

Among the most important inventions in the field of mass communication are radio and television. Though successful experiments in transmitting radio signals and visuals had been carried out towards the end of 19th century, full-fledged radio broadcasting centres in United States and many European countries were set up in the first half of 20th century followed by television stations after a few years. Historically speaking, in many countries radio broadcasts have been used for rural development and education. During the second world war radio was extensively used for news and for war propaganda. Generally, the television centres adopted similar approach though with greater proportion of light entertainment programmes.

In the preceding few decades, revolutionary changes have taken place in communication technology. The satellites have facilitated worldwide communication transcending national boundaries; mass communication has effectively been internationalized. This has enabled the technologically developed nations to dominate information networks. Multi-national organisations have got into a position of influencing social, cultural, economic and political life in the under-developed countries. In fact, media imperialism of the capitalist west is a component of cultural, political and economic imperialism.

THE INDIAN SITUATION

The number of radio stations in India has expanded tremendously after country attained independence. From only six stations in 1947 the present network covers nearly 99 per cent of population. According to latest annual report of Prasar Bharati, the broadcasting corporation of radio and television, radio network covers nearly 93 per cent of country's area and 99 per cent of population. It comprises 146 medium wave, 54 short wave and 161 frequency modulation transmitters; a total of 361. However, this is only indicative of technical coverage. Reportedly, there are still many gray areas where radio signal is either extremely weak or is not received. On the other hand, some foreign broadcasting stations have clear and strong signal strength and command considerable listenership particularly in regions bordering with other countries. In recent times, the situation seems to have improved considerably with the availability of satellites. The network of television centres has also expanded to cover almost the entire country. The fact, however, remains that in spite of tremendous increase in the ownership of radio and television sets, many people still do not have direct access to radio or TV broadcasts.

DEVELOPMENT COMMUNICATION

Development involves both social change and economic growth. Development communication refers to the process by which mass media are used to promote development. Countries like India have been trying to tackle the problems of hunger, poverty, illiteracy, unemployment, social inequality, etc. with programmes of planned change and development. In this regard, many scholars from western countries have recommended various models and approaches for development. Among these, the media centric approach has received maximum attention. It lays emphasis on expanding mental horizons, promoting literacy, hastening the process of urbanisation and making people aware of technological and economic advancement in developed countries. The proponents of this approach feel that efforts should be directed to make people aspire for better quality of life and encourage them to raise their income levels to achieve it. For this, mass media networks needed to be expanded to a level where information becomes a major component in moving people towards development. In their opinion, mass media could act as 'catalysts of change', 'magic multipliers', 'magic bullet or a hypodermic needle' in reaching appropriate information to target audiences. In this paradigm, tremendous power has been attributed to mass media in initiating the processes of social change and economic development. However, experience with development communication in the past has shown that mass media are no panacea for all the problems related to development. There can be far more powerful agents of change as well as barriers to it. The Indian experience with educational television and development oriented programmes has shown that inspite of its tremendous potential the media could not achieve the level of expected success. The initial euphoria with the novelty of experiment, as indicated by enthusiasm of the audiences, was short lived. The large appreciative audience, some how or the other, failed to put into practice the knowledge they had got from the media. The very high level of awareness about various development schemes resulted in rather low level of adoption. There could be a variety of factors of diverse origin and nature acting as barriers to behavioural changes. Various studies in this field have shown that environmental constraints, lack of resources, group resistance, rumours and misconceptions, social and cultural barriers, lack of proper understanding or misinterpretation of intended information, etc. were some of the factors dissuading people from adopting the new practices.

It is noteworthy that there would always be a gap between potential of a medium as instrument of social change and progress, and its effectiveness in real life situations. Effective use of media for development depends on the administrative ethos, the operational realities at the implementation level and social setting within which the information is received. Communication is one of a wide range of factors which determine the audience response. Changes in attitudinal and normative behaviours are seldom unifactorial or unidirectional. In tradition bound societies, every individual is an integral part of a social system, product of a culture and, as such, his/her behaviour is determined by the group to which he/she it belongs. It has been observed in the past that even when a person was attitudinally convinced of the utility of a programme, he/she could not adopt it because of group pressure. Audiences are dynamic participants in the process of communication. Their response, to a great extent, depends on institutional setting, social symbiosis, inter group interlinkages, level of social and economic development, access to mass media, group dynamics, leadership and village organisation.

As the media environment changes, so do people and societies. It is, therefore, difficult to follow the complex processes of communication and diffusion. Mass communication is a component of larger societal process of control, adaptation and integration. Media and its audience together make a system. Every aspect of communication has a cultural dimension; since society and culture are interdependent, they mutually reinforce each other. The degree of dependence on media systems is contingent on the type of information sought and dependability of the medium as a credible source of information. Effects of mass media communication can be properly understood only within the cultural realities like tradition, values, beliefs and practices. Audience composition and level of their interest may vary by the cultural contexts and social influences. Society is an organic whole with well defined structures, functions and social institutions. Social life evolves constantly and with that the social relationships also undergo changes. Social systems provide the matrix for communication while social changes takes place through inter systemic interactions and according to individual or group goals.

Communication from exogenous sources undergoes a process of internal validation. Peoples' response to it depends on cognitive complexity, mental projections as relevant to personal issues and also the level of apathy because of redundent or irrelevant information. In the tradition bound societies, communication over mass media passes through two or multi step flows and thereafter trickles down through interpersonal or intergroup interactions. Limited reach of mass media in the underdeveloped societies forces people to fall back upon their own sources of information or the indigenous interactional communication systems. Implicitly much of their information, knowledge and understanding about different issues depends on the interpretation by their own sources. In such situations, diffusion of information through interactional channels is generally confined to respective groups. It also depends on the social and economic statuses as there may be inequalities in access to media communication. People receive information within their own communication environment. The trickle down process of messages is never random but flows through established channels as defined by social structure. Changes in normative behaviours cannot be brought about independent of structural factors. In India, rural societies have hierarchical social stratification comprising various castes and communities. These live separately as close knit entities, follow group determined behaviour and inter group relations which influence patterns of intercommunication, and dissemination of information. With communication passing through multiple filters, there would always be likelihood of distortions in the intended message at the level of target audience.

The dynamics of culture change is influenced by technology, ethno-religious considerations, social economy and political commitments. There is a process of rationalisation and social legitimisation of new behaviour to minimise crises intrinsic to exogenously induced changes. People devise ways to adopt and adjust to changing social environment. Social situation is never static and continuously necessitates adoptive behaviours for maintaining social equilibrium, while emergent new institutions compound the structural complexity. Social action cannot be understood merely in terms of individual attitudes ignoring the fact that these are themselves product of socio-economic conditions, power relationships and socio-cultural traditions. Ideas cannot be manipulated independent of structural factors nor can they be foisted by ignoring the socio-cultural realities. Development demands greater efforts in pursuit of equality. Broad aggregate indices of development have little relevance for poverty ridden people. Illiterate and poor people have survival as their only priority in life. For them development in terms of import of technology, capital formation, urbanization, etc. have little relevance. In their constant struggle to manage two square meals a day, they tend to minimize conflicts with their social, cultural, political or economic environment. They prefer to flow with the tide and in the process become status quoists or often resistant to change.

In India, in spite of over five decades of sustained developmental effort, peoples' response to many programmes has remained much below expectations. The tendency has been to accept those programmes which can ensure quick and direct benefits. Thus even a very high degree of awareness has not resulted in corresponding behavioural changes. The possible reasons for this situation could be:

1. low perceived utility of the development programmes;
2. lack of cultural compatibility and perspective in presenting messages making it difficult for the target audience to empathize with the situation; and
3. a cognitive hiatus about need of a programme as visualised by policy planners and as perceived by the people.

The above is indicative of the failure of communication effort to generate favourable attitudes, remove doubts and misconceptions and counteract resistances. The communication approach has generally remained model synchronic, programme specific but seldom based on specific information needs of the people. This strategy is not suited to situations where inter-communication is generally ethnocentric and decision making a group function. Social transformation takes place when all the supporting factors have highest probability of occurring at a point of time and which can cumulatively result in the desired change. Likewise development with mass media as catalysts would be possible when all the other relevant factors are favourable.

Considering the element of ethno-linguistic and socio-cultural heterogeneity in India, overcentralization in development communication may not be effective. The processes of communication and diffusion being far too complex and structural factors far too varied, there cannot be universal solutions for local issues. The need is to adopt a culture area approach. The dynamics of social change calls for a dynamic communication approach which, in turn, depends on an equally dynamic research and feed back system.

COMMUNICATION RESEARCH

Most of the researches in the field of mass communication have been ivory tower investigations carried out within assumptions which have seldom been empirically tested. The impact of media communication on human behaviour is generally measured as relationship between independent and dependent variables with mass media being treated as independent variable. This is over-simplification of a very complex process. It implies that media communication and resultant behavioural changes can be understood in terms of relationship between variables or simple mathematical correlations. Taking individual as the unit of analysis disregards the fact that decision making in tradition bound societies is a group function and there can be several nuclei of decision making based on kinship, caste, community, factions or the interest groups.

Academic and professional research in the field of mass communication in India, generally speaking, coincides with the launching of programmes of planned development in early Fifties. The period beginning 1950 is significant for the fact that fundamental changes were taking place in the country with profound impact on social, cultural, economic and political life. Constitution of India guaranteed equal opportunity and rights to all of its citizens irrespective of caste or creed. Landlord - tenant cultivator system had been abolished in many parts of the country. Elected councils of village people replaced the institution of village headman. Community Development Programme was launched for which peoples' participation was sought through extension agencies and mass media. With the result basic changes were taking place in the institutional structures of rural society.

In the initial stages, studies were carried out by social scientists to study dynamics of social transformation in the rural communities. By and large, these studies were academic in nature and concerned more with the processes of change. Study of group dynamics, patterns of interaction and communication were incidental in such researches. The other major contribution during this period was the studies carried out by extension agencies with main focus on community mobilization, role of leaders and acceptance of innovations. Subsequently, the focus of researchers shifted to family planning communication and later to effects of mass media communication, particularly television. During this period many researchers also studied the possible use of audio and video cassettes as aid to small group communication. The analysis of general trends in communication research over a period of five decades shows that there had been a constant shift in the focus of studies. Starting with interactional communication in the form of village studies, the interest of researchers shifted to attitudinal studies of acceptors of development programmes. There was again a movement towards study of mass media communication with the expansion in the network of television centres. During this period some scholars also studied the use of video technology for small group communication and education. The changing fashions in research in a way necessitated a constant change in the units of study. Starting with the village communities for assessing structural changes in the society, processes of communication and diffusion, adoption of innovations. Attention later shifted to individuals as unit of study, their attitudinal and normative behaviours. The focus again shifted to family as a unit of study as most of development communication, though meant for larger population group, was essentially directed to family as the unit. Programmes like small savings, health, insurance, family planning, etc. were meant for the whole family. Subsequently, the attention again shifted to village studies for assessing the impact of television and resultant social change.

A few points arising out of an overview of communication research merit attention:

Band Wagon Approach

Generally speaking there had not been a balanced approach in carrying out communication researches. There had always been a mass movement of researchers from one field to the other. The scramble towards new fashions in research has resulted in imbalances as also neglect of many important programme areas. Because of lack of proper research support, the mediated communication for development became repetitive with the result there was redundancy of information on the one hand and gaps in knowledge of the target audience on the other. While almost all the monetary support to communication research, directly or indirectly was provided by the government, by and large, these efforts remained lopsided.

Greater importance to Medium than the Message

Researches related to mass media in many cases have focused more on the carrier of messages such as television, video technology or radio than on the content of messages. The communication technology assumed the role of master in such situations than the message or target audience.

Inadequate assessment of Models and Theories

Majority of models and theories pertaining to development were evolved in the countries where socio-cultural and economic determinants were basically different from the Indian situation. The demand creation models developed in the field of commercial advertising were more suited to highly individualistic affluent societies where people generally had direct access to sources of information and also had necessary resources to take follow up action. In comparison in India, the kin-group, caste or community exercises considerable influence over individuals. Besides, many people do not have direct access to sources of information. Poverty and lack of resources also prevent people from making use of available facilities. The communication researchers in India, however, have not tried to assess the applicability of available communication models in the Indian situation. On the other hand, a large number of studies have been carried out to collect information which fits into the available models.

Lack of Methodological Innovations

Interlinked with the general diffidence in assessing the applicability as utility of available models and theories, is the general lack of initiative to generate indigenous models and theories based on Indian experience. The result is that majority of researches conform to a set pattern and provide information on what is already known.

Lack of Understanding of Indigenous Communication System

Efforts have not been made to understand the structure and organization of the indigenous interactional communication systems in the rural areas. Strong social ties lead to group's influence over individual members which in a way curbs their initiative and capacity to take independent decisions. Much of the effectiveness of mediated communication as a matter of fact, depends on the extent of participation by the local channels. This, however, has remained a neglected area of research.

REFERENCES

1. Stanley Baran, Davis and K. Dennis, *Mass Communication, Theory,* (2002).
2. Paul Hartman, B.R. Patil and Anita Dighe, *Media and Village Life,* (1992).
3. P.C. Joshi, *Communication and National Development,* (2002).
4. Daniel Lerner and Wilbur Schramm, *Communication and Change in the Developing Countries,* (1967).
5. Sunil Misra, *Overview of Communication Research in India,* (1989).
6. Sunil Misra, *Voluntary Action in Health and Population: Dynamics of Social Transition,* (2002).
7. A.V. Shanmugham, *Communication Research in India,* (1983).

10

Conflict Zone Photography – The Third Eye

Manish Swarup

World has seen two full-fledged wars in 20th century and has in the past witnessed numerous battles. The world today has conflict and combat zones where various groups are warring for rights or land. War photography depicts the horrors and terrors of war mingled with selfless acts of sacrifice of soldiers. A war photograph denotes something more than images of battle or combat. It can refer to military photographs, prisoners of war pictures, grieving soldiers or even images of civilians injured in cross fire or caught in the middle of conflict.

War photographers try to capture the images of armed conflicts as well as life in war torned areas. These photographers have to be adventurous, restless and prepared to face hardships. Unlike reporters, who can report a story from a certain 'safe' distance, a photographer must get to the scene of action, whatever the danger or discomfort. Nothing can stand between him and the reality of happening. He has to be at the right place at the right time. No re-write desk can save him. His picture happens to be the last word, having lasting impact.

Just like a rain shower affects the water level in the mighty ocean, a photograph can impact the flow of history, shape public perception and opinion on changing course of human attitudes and lives. For instance, the photograph during the Vietnam War that showed several children including an eight year old girl running with her burning clothes torn off, after American planes dropped napalm bombs on south Vietnamese troops and civilians, became symbolic of civilian suffering in Vietnam, thereby discrediting government account of the war. It roused public sentiment which eventually forced the government to withdraw from the war.

Conflict photographers often place themselves in the mouth of danger to get a story or a photo. Although, photographers and journalists are protected by international conventions of armed warfare, warring groups often consider them as soft targets for trade offs or simply to show their hatred for the opponent. History has claimed many photographers and journalists, abducted and executed by terrorists for a distant cause. War photography has become more dangerous with the terrorist style of armed conflict.

While photography in such conflict zones involves life and death, blood and gore and plenty of drama, the photographer becomes a professional voyeur. He wants to capture action, danger and drama directed by at someone else for him to be able to shoot at a 'safe' distance. In 1936, Robert Capa's photograph of a Spanish Republican soldier, caught in the moment of death became such a controversial image that Capa came to hate it.

While on the scene, the photographer busies himself with the job, emotion hits him later. The realization that he/she was veering on the thin road between life and death, the smell of bombing, shooting and killing that one witnessed; grief of the people and utter hopelessness of the situation clings on to him/her until next assignment.

I have been on assignment to Kashmir, Kargil, post war Kosovo during the UN occupation-besides Afghanistan, Iraq, Sri Lanka and Nepal, a few hot spots of the Asian world. My experience in Kargil, Afghanistan, Iraq and even Nepal was every time different, but every experience helped me to cover the next one better.

KARGIL

I went to Kargil in June 1999, when the Indo-Pak battle was at its peak. We were positioned with the Indian Army at Drass, the mountainous battleground for an undeclared war between India and Pakistan. Stillness of the evening air crackled with tension and we knew something major was about to happen. Rocket launchers and Bofors guns were taking positions. The Army was moving for a frontal attack against the militants on Tiger Hill.

Within minutes, firing started. The Indian guns opened their mouth to let out a quick burst of flame with shells travelling at a speed of more than 500 kilometres an hour which burst in a frenzy of fire several kilometres away.

The flames lit up the faces of the artillerymen. Their faces reflected waves of immense patriotic joy. Their chests thrust forward with pride especially when the surveyor, armed with powerful binoculars announced, "Good fire boys, right on target". It is an unforgettable memory. Even the light drizzle had stopped, as if because of the force of the Indian fire.

Meanwhile, hungry for action, we were clicking away with a mad frenzy. With each focused click of the shutter, it felt like even we had targeted the enemy. Never having seen fighting like this from such close quarters, it was easy in a stray moment to feel that this was an India-Pakistan cricket match. Bullets continued to whiz past us as we took more pictures of rocket launchers.

Night fell. The firing continued. We decided to travel to Kargil from where we could file our news and pictures for people hungry for information from the border. But while our car was just outside the brigade headquarters at Drass, the first shell from the Pak side landed just 200 metres ahead of our car. As we saw the burst of flame and splinters flying, we knew this was serious. It was battlefront, not a cricket match. Everybody ran towards the bunkers nearby.

Another shell landed, somewhere close. We could repeatedly hear the *Dhudooooom* of the shellfire. There was near panic as journalists dashed towards the bunkers for safety. The survival instinct was strong.

I too quickly ducked under the cover of a bunker. There was a lull for a few seconds. This was broken with the voice of a jawan who announced, "A journalist was hurt."

I immediately looked out for Rajesh, our correspondent and found him missing. Worried, I ran out as one of the soldiers quickly walked into the bunker with Rajesh, holding onto his side.

I made Rajesh as comfortable as possible with his head on my lap, in the small bunker of six people where there were already 10 persons now. Shells kept falling endlessly. All the journalists, except the jawans, started praying. These fearless jawans were our self-appointed protectors.

I casually half asked, half commented, "I hope these bunkers are shell proof?"

"Sorry sir, these bunkers are only splinter proof", a jawan replied. "If a shell falls on this bunker, we will have to take another life", he said.

"Just three days back, a shell fell on one of the bunkers and we found the remnants of three jawans, who were inside", he continued.

His voice still echoes in my memory and goose pimples run up my arms when I realise how close to the edge of life all of us were in that small bunker that cold night in Drass. We prayed, even more fervently, if that was possible, that no shell should fall on the bunker. Thoughts of family and loved ones back home flitted into the mind.

We could see shells falling outside our bunker. Miraculously none fell on the bunker but all around it. After about an hour of shelling, we decided to move Rajesh to the MI, medical room, a little away from our bunker.

It was pitch dark outside. We heard more shells while going towards the MI room, where a doctor, who somehow inspired confidence and faith, asked us to go back to a bunker and leave Rajesh with him.

Within the cocoon of the bunker, each time we heard shell fire, we asked whose side was it from: India or Pakistan. Each time we were told, it was the Indian side. This, whether true or false, was quite heartening news.

In the middle of this battleground, the brave men of the Army offered us hot rice and *dal* and a vegetable. They gave us sleeping bags to stretch our legs.

Interestingly, we learnt that the men from signals ensured that the telephone lines were working on the mountains. Every time a party went uphill to combat the militants, one of the signals men would accompany them, to ensure communication with the base camp. They were constantly in the line of fire.

Every time a contact had to be made, it was through the World War II phones, which I was surprised to learn, were still working. These phones did not have the disconnector button. Instead they were activated by the receiver end being beaten on the body of the phone, three four times in quick succession, *thak thak thak*. The phone body had a key, which had to be turned several times to activate a ring in the corresponding phone. The longer it was keyed, the stronger would be the ring at the other end. Then one had to yell to be heard at the other end.

In the morning, when I woke up, all was quiet. Out of the bunker, I found that our jeep driver was safe but the jeep was damaged. A splinter, about the size of a large matchbox, had flown through the roof of the jeep, burnt its way through the seats and through the floor of the jeep into the ground and back up through the floor of the vehicle and down to the ground again. I was astounded at the power of a small burning iron splinter travelling at over 700 km per hour.

It had been an eventful night. I saw some of the jawans in Drass being photographed singing and dancing with joy and delight and repeatedly making the victory sign. Their joy was contagious and it doubled when I learnt that the tigers had captured Tiger Hill, a major hideout of the militants. Tiger Hill was ours again. The country's boundaries were recaptured.

Meanwhile, the good doctor had operated on Rajesh during the night, and this journalist was on his way to recovery. The doctor had also operated on two soldiers during the night, and arranged for a blood transfusion for one of them. In absolute makeshift conditions, he had saved the life of the soldier after a six hour-long operation. He had been up from 1 AM the previous day up to 10 PM that night. All in a day's work.

The army doctors had lost count of the operations they had performed and the lives they had saved. I saw that the canvas of the tents, in which the patients were kept, was shredded by hundreds of splinters. I realised then that in this rough, uncertain terrain, all men were equal, the doctors were God and only the God was the Saviour.

BAGHDAD, IRAQ

Before going to any assignment, especially in a foreign land, while it is important to know the geography of the land, the prevailing political situation, areas of conflict and areas of peace, it is more important to respect these warnings. In a war situation, one knows the enemy but in a conflict zone, dangers are everywhere. Hence, it is also helpful to do a crash course on local culture as well as homework on the quality of interaction between dominant groups.

I recall I had to travel from Jordan border to Baghdad by road, an 11-12 hour drive. I was wearing a bulletproof jacket travelling in a BMW car with my translator and driver, Sadiq and carrying about US $50,000. Sadiq warned me that we would not stop anywhere on the way as the area is known for shoot-outs, kidnapping and carjackers. Danger was perceived even from an overtaking vehicle. We passed areas where the militia was strong and Sadiq told me how a BBC vehicle, just the other day, was attacked and journalists taken as hostage. The only thing I could do was pray that the drive might pass eventlessly.

On my first visit to Iraq, I was there for nearly two months. In spite of the dangers, I loved shooting daily life in Iraq following the American invasion. The people were generally warm and welcomed Indians. However, I soon discovered that this bonhomie was only an illusion, providing me with a false sense of security.

I remember shooting in a hardline mosque, where only Muslims were permitted. Two or three bearded persons came to me and asked about my religion. Sadiq, my translator managed the situation by saying, "he is not very good Muslim as he does not offer *namaaz*" and we both came out fast. It was later on that I learnt that mosque did not permit entry to non-Muslims.

I also got the opportunity to stay for a couple of days with the American army. It was not easy shooting from within. There were restrictions on movement and for every picture, we had to seek permission, which was not easily forthcoming, probably because I was an Asian. I could not risk shooting without permission. I learnt that recently US soldiers shot a Reuter's cameraman as he was focusing his camera towards American soldiers in a tank. With a long lens hanging from the neck, a photographer may, form a distance, look like a militant wielding a rocker launcher.

During my subsequent visits to Iraq, I found that the city had gone from bad to worse. Earlier the attacks were mainly against the army. Three years later, general public was being targeted and there were frequent kidnappings too. I was therefore required to remain in a well-guarded, fortified residence cum office and be the Photo Editor, who never stepped out into the city but worked vicariously through local photographers.

Once, there was a bomb blast close to our office. I gave my camera and lens to the local photographer, who was not carrying his own. He was one of the first to reach the site. And paid a price for it. Iraqi police took away the camera and lens from him on gunpoint and smashed it in front of his eyes. He received a beating too. It was frustrating not to be where the action was.

I worked through each day as it brought more and more senseless violence. In one single day, hundreds of lives were destroyed in car bombings and roadside bomb explosions at the city's oldest wholesale market while in the south of Baghdad, an explosive rigged bicycle detonated near an army recruiting centre. Insurgents often targeted Iraqi army and police volunteers as they waited outside recruiting stations, as a way to discourage people from joining the security services. Even children were not spared. A bomb that exploded was placed outside a school.

Tensions between the Shias and Sunnis were mounting. The security crisis in Iraq was turning more complex with Sunni insurgents fighting American troops in the west, Sunnis and Shiites killing one another in Baghdad and then Shiites battling Shiites in south of Iraq.

All bloodshed and brutality of a conflict zone affects one's spirit. There happens to be uneasiness in the air, in one's interaction with the local people. One simply wants to shoot and scoot. One happens to be there to record glimpses of life, not there to spy or pass judgement on a people or culture.

KABUL, AFGHANISTAN

As our plane started its descent on Kabul, it was a scene just out of a picture book. A white bed cover of snow seemed to be draped over this rugged and hardy city. It looked like a painting. But when we landed, the ground reality was totally different, just like the city. The ground was watery and slippery, clods of dust pockmarked the pristine snow, the luggage belt at the airport did not work and there were no trolleys. Outside, the temperature was –3 degrees and the chilly wind zoomed into the ears and head. But the bonhomie and warmth of an Afghani welcome, with smiles glittering like jewels through the stubble and beards, made us forget all inconveniences.

I have been to Afghanistan three times on assignment and each time it was a different kind of fascinating experience. On my last visit in January 2007, driving out of the airport, I could see municipal employees working at clearing the snow. Poverty was still openly visible, Traffic had increased manifold and I could see children playing football on the ice instead of being at school. Still, things looked more in control than during my previous visits to Kabul.

Being the capital city, Kabul was relatively safe but towards south Afghanistan, where the Taliban have a strong base, one has to be very careful. There is a high risk of being abducted, shot or executed. Therefore, I had to go through the local leader or the town head. However, with the political changes underway, at least in Kabul I could sense that people have started to move out of the control of the Taliban. They can taste the power and consequently given the poverty, bribery and corruption are on the rise. The respect for Indians too is on the decline.

On assignment in Afghanistan, I also found the presence of the American and British Army restrictive because if you are with the army, you cannot shoot the locals and vice versa.

Shooting women was a different ballgame altogether. I found it effective to go through the local NGOs. But I still had to be fast and careful while taking pictures of women in *burqua*. It was fascinating to watch scores of women wearing electric blue *burqua*s thronging the market place, veils firmly in place. How do their husbands recognise them? I wondered. Apparently, husbands recognised their wives through the footwear.

In my last visit, I was embedded with the British troops and moved with them on their attack projects to destabilise the Taliban. But prior to being posted at a base in interior part of Afghanistan, we had a briefing by the British Press Officer in the army. We were told about the reconstruction work being conducted. Opium production was being controlled; schools and hospitals had been started with the help of local NGOs. Locals are being recruited for training in the army to enable them to fight the Taliban. The aim was to make the Taliban inconsequential.

I was posted at Camp Bastion, the largest British camp in the middle of the desert. Wearing the heavy but compulsory gear of bulletproof jackets and helmets, we boarded the British Royal Air Force Hercules C-130 plane in the evening and one half hours later landed at Camp Bastion in total darkness, lights were not used because of security reasons. The local name of the British camp Bastion was *Dasht-e-Margo* or 'the desert of death.' It housed some 3500 British servicemen and provided logistic support to all the troops for their various operations in Southern Afghanistan.

Bastion was a big camp, situated bang in the middle of the desert. It was also our base from where we flew out on operations. For miles, one could see only fine sand. Anybody approaching the camp from any side could be spotted miles away. I lived in a heated tent, meant for 10 people, that I shared with another cameraman. For toilets and shower, the British Army had converted a container into baths and toilets, all fitted with warmers with hot and cold water available 24 x 7.

A couple of days later, we left for Kajaki, a forward base of the British forces. Kajaki is the place where Afghanistan has the biggest water reservoir and a dam, which provides water and electricity to millions of people. The Taliban had obstructed its operations.

We flew to Kajaki in a Chinook helicopter. The landscape was mystical. Barren mountains surrounded by desert with no vegetation for miles and then suddenly in the middle of the mountain was this huge lake with crystal clear water, reflecting the rugged, craggy mountains.

The Kajaki camp of the British Army did not offer the same luxurious facilities. It was bitterly cold. There was no heated tent and no running water and only makeshift toilets made of wooden benches. One had to aim and piss in pipes.

We had the opportunity to participate in an Army operation, a few miles away from camp. We moved with five British soldiers under the orders of the camp's second in command.

About 100 soldiers were involved in this operation to weed out the Taliban from desert strongholds. We started early in the morning at around 04:00 hours and marched to the attack site about 4 kilometres away near a hill next to a village. About 100 soldiers quietly creeped into the village to weed out the Taliban. We watched and zoomed into the action from the hill to get our pictures.

The landscape offered the Taliban excellent protection. But the British soldiers in several rounds of heavy firing with sophisticated weapons shot and killed about 14 Taliban men. With the extra men on board, we were told to walk 4 kilometres along a dried up river bed wearing our bulky bullet proof jackets and helmet and lugging heavy cameras, lens and photography equipment. I can never forget that long walk to safety with two attack helicopters Apaches flying in the sky for the safety of the troops.

Our next assignment was at Sparwan Ghar, 40 kilometres west of Kandahar in the Taliban belt. We spent four days here. At 18:00 hours, a British officer informed us that Sparwan Ghar was a forward operating base and we would be leaving at 23:15 hours by road with the Canadian army convoy and then on to the final destination. The thought of a four-hour journey in the night, along a dangerous route infested with militants and prone to IED attacks was not exactly comforting.

Just before departure, at the convoy point, we were briefed about the situation and the action to be taken in case of a ground attack or if any vehicle was hit by an IED. We were informed that one week ago, the convoy got an IED and suicide bomber attack, although no one was injured. My heart was heavy and my faith was strong.

We sat in the second vehicle, closed from all sides with no window. There was just one hole where the gunner stood. He was an Indian, but a Canadian National, working for the Canadian Army.

We rolled out sharp on time, passed Kandahar town and then hit the highway. Sleep was as far away from my mind as the distance between the sun and planet Pluto. The human mind is so devious that one only thinks those thoughts that one does not want to touch. Every bump and turn made me extra alert.

We finally reached the Canadian base, our first destination, by 01:00 hours without any untoward incident. When we came out of the vehicle, it was pitch dark. We were in the lap of a mountain and could see their tall silhouette against a black velvet sky studded with thousands of stars. It was an amazing sight and in that moment, I felt no fear, just wonder. I have never seen so many stars before. But the temperature was freezing.

Meanwhile, the soldiers were unloading equipment from the tanks and other containers. The entire exercise took place in the dark, with no light, just a small red light torch.

A lady officer offered us some coffee and we were taken to a bomb shelter and later to a heated tent that was their kitchen, where we had more coffee. After nearly an hour, we moved into the convoy commander's vehicle, as our vehicle had broken down. This was a huge bullet proof South African made, state of art armoured vehicle with a gunner inside the vehicle equipped with a night vision screen and a joystick, which was the trigger of a heavy machine gun. This was totally unlike our earlier vehicle where the gunner had to sit on the vehicle in the open.

However, the convoy commander's vehicle was the first one in the convoy, which meant it was the first target. It was comforting to know that vehicle was fitted with big bulletproof windows, and we could see outside.

It made a big difference to be able to see the road and not sit cooped up in a dark vehicle, not knowing when some Taliban may spring up with a rocket launcher.

Finally an hour later, we reached our final destination Sparwan Ghar at 3.30 AM. It was a base of British, US and Canadian forces. We crashed out on wooden bunked beds and slept like dogs.

At Sparwan ghar, formerly the Taliban belt of southern Afghanistan, we visited schools and hospitals started by the troops and saw the social work being done by the troops, giving a humane face to the area which had earlier witnessed only atrocities committed in this war torn country.

It was only after return to main camp that I had a bath. Four days later. I had sand sticking to my body, my moustache and hair. No words can describe the sensation of standing under warm water and feeling each and every tiny particle of sand sliding down your body.

CONFLICT ZONES ARE NOT TOURIST SPOTS

I have also been to Nepal on assignment to cover the people's struggle for freedom from monarchy besides covering militancy in Kashmir and terrorism in Sri Lanka. One needs to be prepared for a rough life while in conflict zones. One needs to watch for land mines, explosives, suicide bombings, gas, shootouts and anything else that makes a conflict zone dangerous.

I remember I lost a dear friend and colleague, an excellent photographer from *Hindustan Times*, Pradeep Bhatia, in Kashmir. He was the first to reach the site of a car bomb explosion. As soon as he took the photos, another car nearby exploded and he was instantly killed.

Conflict zone photography also helps to understand the political and economic environment and culture of the local people. One needs to go there prepared with contacts, friends, NGOs, etc. Conflict zones are certainly not tourist destinations for vacationing people going for pleasure and relaxation.

11

Information Requirements of a Modern Democracy

I. Ramamohan Rao

The communication skills of people of India are centuries old, but the government information dissemination system in India has been fashioned by the colonial rulers and it has not yet completely recovered from the hangover.

The colonial rulers never felt that it was their responsibility to keep the people of India informed about their actions. The East India Company's efforts were mostly directed at suppressing information from reaching newspapers. J.A. Hickey, the publisher of the first English newspaper in India, the Bengal Gazette, which started in January 1780 – was prosecuted and imprisoned. It was considered beneath the Government's dignity to give information to the Press.

The East India Company and later the British Government could not stop the growth of the Press in India. The number of newspapers steadily grew, and so also their influence. In an effort to control them, the Government passed the notorious Vernacular Press Act in 1878. The duties of the 'Press Officer' were to suppress information rather than give information to the Press.

The need for some machinery to interact with the press was felt during the First World War, as thousands of Indian soldiers joined the British Indian Army and fought in various theatres of war, including Europe, North Africa and Middle East. There was need to disseminate information to the families of the soldiers, and also keep the recruitment effort continuing. Publicity Boards were set up in the country with a Central Publicity Board under the Home Member.

At the end of the War, the Government found no need for interacting with newspapers. The main function of the Bureau of Information – set up in 1923 – was restricted to prepare a report on India to be presented to the Secretary of State in London. The colonial administration in India only felt that its responsibility was over by reporting to the British Government, and in turn the British Parliament.

The newspapers reported the happenings in the country, gave space to orders issued by the administration, but had little or no access to people who formulated policies.

Meanwhile, the demand for self-government was gathering momentum. The British Government had to respond and initiatives were taken to hold a Round Table Conference in London. With the passing of the Government of India Act 1935, the need was felt for the setting up of an information disseminating system in India.

The existing Bureau of Information was recast and its head was designated the Principal Information Officer in 1938. The task of the Bureau was to present material in the form required by the Press – as news stories.

The Bureau of Information started functioning in the late thirties. India was again forced to participate in the British war effort. Unlike World War I, the Congress Party opposed the participation of India in the war, unless the country was promised freedom.

The office of the Commander-in-Chief set up its own department for Public Relations. Public Relations Officers were deputed to various formations in different theatres of war and their reports were collected and released to various newspapers. Cameramen, both still and audio-visual, were sent to cover the war. Their dispatches were collected, edited and shown in cinema theatres. The Films Division in Bombay processed them.

During World War II, the Bureau of Public Information became responsible for publicizing the activities of the Government as also to counter the anti-British propaganda. The Government had to deal with the language press as also the freedom movement which had gathered momentum.

The government found it necessary to engage the services of Indian journalists to cover its activities. J. Natarajan was the first Indian to be appointed the Principal Information Officer. The Bureau of Public Information, in turn, was renamed as the Press Information Bureau.

Independent India, which adopted the British system of parliamentary democracy, needed an effective system to disseminating information to the people. Our founding fathers, who were great communicators and had mobilized The Government of India strengthened the Press Information Bureau, the All India Radio, the Films Division, and the Publications Division. The Directorate of Public Relations of the Ministry of Defence became a part of the Press Information Bureau.

All organizations responsible for information work were brought under the newly created Ministry of Information and Broadcasting. The Government issued a manual of office procedure which directed that all 'news' should be communicated to the Press though the Press Information Bureau and that the 'information officer' will become the official spokesman to the press and that he should have access to all sources of information. The Information Officer was to be briefed by senior officials from time to time.

The Press Information Bureau opened offices in almost all State capitals of the country. Teleprinters were linked, and regional branch officers of the PIB translated the releases made in Delhi and sent them to the language newspapers. In addition, till recently, publicity material, including photographs, used to be sent to different offices of the PIB located in State capitals and important press centres through air bags.

In the initial stages the Government was mostly concerned with the maintenance of law and order. In the fifties, the Government of Independent India embarked on the task of planned development. For the success of different programmes, there was a need to create awareness of projects and make the people partners in their implementation.

The Government of India set up the Directorate of Field Publicity, which was entrusted with the task of mobilizing the people of the country to support development programmes through inter-personal communication. The Directorate of Advertising and Visual Publicity, the Exhibition Division and the Song and Drama Division came into being in the early fifties.

The All India Radio, which was founded in 1936, today has a network of over 215 broadcasting centres covering over 92 per cent of the country. It broadcasts in 24 languages and 146 dialects, through nearly 150 medium wave transmitters, and over 60 frequency modulation transmitters.

Television was started as an experimental set up in the Capital in September 1959. Designated Doordarshan, it expanded in the eighties and presently has transmitters covering nook and corners of the country. It telecasts programmes in all major languages. In the nineties, the Prasar Bharati was created and the Doordarshan and All India Radio were brought under it.

The media scene has changed over the years and, the government information machinery has had to keep pace with the changes. The number of newspapers has grown astronomically. Today, the number of newspapers and periodicals is over 55,000 and still growing. Many newspapers claim circulation of a million or more. The trend is that major newspapers have editions printed simultaneously from many centres.

Till the early 90s, All India Radio and the Doordarshan had a monopoly, but the scene has changed with the arrival of satellite television. They first entered the country in the early nineties during the Gulf War, and have since mushroomed. Television has become a powerful medium for swaying public opinion quickly and effectively.

The Government of India had assisted the newspapers by providing subsidized teleprinter networks to the news agencies, the Press Trust of India and the United News of India. To these news agencies have now been added Asian News International, India's only television news agency. In addition, many private channels have their own communications network. Indian news agencies have arrangements with foreign news agencies and they provide news from abroad to the Indian newspapers and television channels and vice-versa.

The Press Information Bureau has had to keep pace with the advances in information technology. Computer networks have now linked all its offices and information and photographs are today available almost simultaneously all over the country, through the National Informatics Centre network.

The different states in the country have also set up their own information organizations similar to the Press Information Bureau. They are generally called the Directorates of Information and they serve the newspapers in the languages of the States they represent.

However, it has taken a great deal of effort to bring about a change in the mindset of the bureaucracy, which has been reluctant to part with information barring a few exceptions. An elder colleague of mine, Mr. H.Y. Sharada Prasad, once mentioned that more effort is spent in the government in filtering information than in giving it. By the time a file reaches from the section officer to the Secretary of the Department, the notings become smaller and smaller and the final version is colourless and odourless.

In response to public demand for getting more information, the Government of India agreed to enact a Right to Information legislation. The Press Council, headed by Justice P.B. Sawant, drafted a Right to Information Legislation in the nineties. Based on this many States and the National Democratic Alliance Government passed Right to Information Bills. But the concerned bureaucracy in the Government of India did not notify the Act with the result that the Act remained on paper.

The United Progressive Alliance passed the Act with a few changes. The Chief Information Commissioner and his team are active and one reads regularly about the war that is waged between the people and the bureaucracy for obtaining information, the most recent being the Judges who do not want to disclose their assets.

Where does one go in appeal?

12

नज़्मः कविता में छपता था यह अखबार!

सूर्यप्रसाद दीक्षित

उफुक लखनवी (श्री द्वारका प्रसाद) ने 5 अगस्त 1888 में लखनऊ से पद्यात्मक भाषा शैली में *नज़्म* नामक पहला उर्दू अख़बार प्रकाशित किया था। भारतीय पत्रकारिता के इतिहास में ही नहीं, संसार की किसी भी भाषा में प्रकाशित होने वाला वह पहला कवित्वपूर्ण अखबार था।

आरंभ में यह अखबार पाक्षिक था, बाद में कुछ दिनों के लिए दैनिक हो गया था। इसमें कुल बारह पृष्ठ हुआ करते थे। चार पन्ने गद्य या नस्र के और आठ पन्ने पद्य के। प्रत्येक अंक के प्रथम पृष्ठ पर एक मसनवी छपा करती थी, जो अखबार की रीति-नीति पर प्रकाश डालती थी। इसका एक उदाहरण द्रष्टव्य है:

है शुक्र उस खालिके आली सिफ़त का
मुसन्निफ है जो वंदेशश जिहत का।
इशाअत नज़्म की करवाई जिसने
दिखायी खूबियां फिक्रेमती की।
गजल तसनीफ की दुनियाओं दी की
कहा खमसा हवासे इन्सो जिनका
किया दीवां मुन्तिब रात दिन का
रक़्म की मसनवीय दीनो ईमां
सुनाई नज़्मे वैदो नसे कुरआं
कहा कता अ चहार अन्फासे तन का।
अनासिर और इखलाते वदन का
बलागत नज़्म परदे में दिखाई
फसाहत नस्र निसरी में दिखाई
रूबाई लिक्खी एतराफे जहां की।

मुंशी द्वारका प्रसाद 'उफुक' लखनऊ के उर्दू कवियों में अग्रगण्य रहे हैं। उनका जन्म 13 जुलाई 1864 को लखनऊ के मोहल्ला नौबस्ता के एक प्रसिद्ध साहित्यिक घराने में हुआ था। उनके परिवार में कई पीढ़ियों से फारसी और उर्दू कविता, साथ ही गद्य लेखन का सिलसिला चला आ रहा था। उनके परदादा थे मुंशी उदयराज 'मतला' जो अपने समय के अच्छे शायर थे। उनके दादा थे - मुंशी ईश्वरी प्रसाद 'खाई'। उन्हें फारसी के अच्छे कवियों में गिना जाता है।

उनके पिता मुंशी पूरनचंद 'जर्रा' को उर्दू गद्य लेखन में पर्याप्त प्रतिष्ठा प्राप्त थी। 'उफुक' के दो बड़े भाई मुंशी रामसहाय 'तमन्ना' और माता प्रसाद 'नैशां' भी उर्दू के अच्छे साहित्यकार माने जाते थे। 'उफुक' के मामा मुंशी शंकर दयाल 'फरहत' ने तुलसी कृत रामायण को फारसी में पद्यबद्ध किया था। उन्हीं से 'उफुक' ने फारसी, अरबी, उर्दू, हिन्दी, संस्कृत, अंग्रेजी आदि भाषाएं सीखीं थीं, साथ ही काव्य कला भी।

अपनी बहुज्ञता के बावजूद 'उफुक' ने उर्दू काव्य और गद्य को अपना क्षेत्र बनाया। वे क्लासिकल साहित्य से लेकर सरल, सुबोध जन साहित्य के लेखन में सक्रिय रहे। उन्होंने लगभग 1100 पृष्ठों में वाल्मीकि की *रामायण* का उर्दू अनुवाद किया। लगभग 2000 पृष्ठों में कर्नल टाड क़ी पुस्तक *एनल्स एण्ड ऐंटीक्विटीज आफ राजपूताना* के 9 खण्ड उन्होंने तैयार किए। इसके बाद *महाभारत, भागवत* के अनुवाद किए। 'उफुक' ने लगभग आधे दर्जन उपन्यास लिखे, जिनमें प्रसिद्ध हैं - *क़ादम्बरी, आलमे तस्वीर, फितना, जुल्फे लैला, शहज़ादी, इन्क़लाब, का* और *तिलिस्म*। इनमें 'उफुक' ने बेगमाती उर्दू का प्रयोग किया है। नाटक के क्षेत्र में भी 'उफुक' बराबर प्रयत्नशील रहे। उनके दो नाटक - *श्रीराम नाटक* और *कृष्ण सुदामा* नाटक अपने समय में बहुत प्रसिद्ध रहे हैं। तीसरा नाटक *भीष्म पितामह* अपूर्ण है। इन नाटकों के बीच पिरोये गए गीत और गज़लें उर्दू पाठकों में मध्य बहुत लोकप्रिय रही हैं।

इस गद्य लेखन के बावजूद यह कहा जा सकता है कि 'उफुक' मूलतः कवि थे। उनकी प्रमुख काव्य कृतियां हैं - 1. *रामायणः यक काफिया*, 2. *रामायण मुसद्दस*, 3. *गज़लों का मजमुआं*, 4. *तीन तवील नज़्में*, 5. *मोरक्कये कमाल*, 6. *मोरक्कये अख़लाक*, 7. *मोरक्कये खयाल*, 8. *सनातन धर्म प्रकाश*, 9. *सवानेह उमरी* (गुरू गोविन्द सिंह खण्ड काव्य), 10. *यादगारे जावेद*, 11. *हयाते बाक़ी*, 12. *नल दमयन्ती* आदि।

उनकी अनेक कृतियां नवल किशोर प्रेस, लखनऊ से प्रकाशित हुई थी। यह समस्त साहित्य इस कथन का प्रमाण है कि 'उफुक' प्रतिभा के धनी थे। कविता में उन्होंने प्रत्येक विधा, जैसे - गज़ल, मुसद्दस, मसनवी, रुबाई, कसीदा, सफरनामा

(यात्रा वृतान्त), हास्य व्यंग्य (तंज़) का प्रयोग किया है। उनकी शायरी में उर्दू ज़बान, बयान और गज़लियत का आनन्द मिलता है।

वस्तुत: लखनऊ के उर्दू स्कूल में उनकी बहुत बड़ी भूमिका रही है। दुर्भाग्यवश गदर के बाद उर्दू मात्र अल्पसंख्यक वर्ग तक सीमित रह गयी। उसमें हिन्दू मिथकों, भारतीय ऐतिहासिक महापुरूषों एवं सांस्कृतिक महत्व वाले उल्लेखों को सम्मिलित करना लगभग वर्जित हो गया। जब उर्दू कविता की मुख्य धारा से ये विषय अलग कर दिए गये तो उर्दू भी यहां अलग थलग पड़ गयी।

उर्दू शायरी से आजीवन सम्बद्ध होने के कारण 'उफुक' अनवरत अपने देशकाल से जुड़े रहे। वे जनजागरण का संदेश देते रहे और उर्दू को नई दिशा की ओर प्रेरित करते रहे। उन्होंने इश्किया शायरी लगभग बंद कर दी। अरबी, फारसी के मिथकों, प्रतीकों, छन्दों और अलंकारों का प्रयोग भी बहुत कम कर दिया। वे जिस युग में लिख रहे थे, उस दौर में लखनवी स्कूल के प्रसिद्ध शायर थे - मोहम्मद हुसैन 'आजाद', हाली, 'दाग', 'आतिश', दबीर, मिर्जा शौक, मुंशी नज़र, हादी रुसवा आदि। 1885 में कांग्रेस की स्थापना हो चुकी थी। 1905 में हुए बंग-भंग से सारा देश लार्ड कर्जन की नीतियों से क्षुब्ध था। डा० इकबाल, चकबस्त, फिराक, जोश मलिहाबादी, अकबर इलाहाबादी, नजीर आदि राष्ट्रीय भाव धारा में पूरी तरह एकाग्र हो गये थे। उल्लेखनीय यह है कि इन सबसे लगभग 40 बर्ष पहले 'उफुक' ने उर्दू की इस नयी शायरी की शुरूआत की थी।

युग बोध और देशप्रेम की भावना ने ही 'उफुक' को पत्रकारिता की ओर प्रेरित किया। उन्होंने अपनी नज़्मों में भरसक सादगी भरी, प्रवाह भरा और जनभाषा का आश्रय लेकर यह काव्यान्दोलन शुरू कर दिया। लखनऊ घराने के प्रमुख कवि होने के कारण 'उफुक' ने लखनवी लहजा, मुहावरेदानी और बंदिशों का प्रयोग किया। उन्होंने नई-पुरानी शायरी को परस्पर जोड़ दिया। सर्वधर्म समभाव या गंगा जमुनी संस्कृति उनके लेखन का मूलोद्‌देश्य बन गयी। कविता पर इस असाधारण अधिकार को देखते हुए निज़ाम हैदराबाद ने उन्हें कविता में अखबार बनाने की सलाह दी और कुछ आर्थिक सहायता भी दी। 'उफुक' ने लखनऊ नौबस्ता में एक छापाखाना 1875 में स्थापित किया और िर शुरू हो गया *नज़्म अखबार*। इस अखबार में समाचार भी कविता में छपता था और विज्ञापन भी। जैसे, एक घटना का यह पद्यात्मक विवरण देखिये-

है उनके शोरोशर से ज़ेर शहजोर
किसी के रोग से दबती नहीं कोर
जफाकारी से बाज आते नहीं हैं
सदा महबे दिन आजारिये ये हैं

किया अहले पुलिस को हाल में तंग
दिखाकर जौहर शमसीरी की जंग।

यह वर्णन दो कालम में छाया हुआ है। पुलिस का दमनचक्र कैसे-कैसे चला? भीड़ ने किस-किस प्रकार से प्रतिरोध किया? सम्पादक ने इसको दंगा न कहकर कौमी शख्सियत का नाम दिया है। कविता में समाचार बनाते हुए विलोम स्टाप, इन्ट्रो उपशीर्षक आदि का निर्वाह नहीं किया गया है, किन्तु घटना का विस्तृत विवरण अवश्य रखा गया है। आवश्यक नाम भी छन्द में 'फिट' कर दिए गये हैं।

वस्तुतः 'उफुक' को छन्द, काफिया, पद विन्यास में पूरी महारत हासिल थी। उसमें आशु कविता और बेतबाजी तथा कव्वाली की तात्कालिक पूर्ति बिठा देने की असाधारण क्षमता थी। गद्य और पद्य दोनों में उनकी समान गति थी। इसलिए वे पद्यात्मक अखबार बनाने में पूर्णतः स्फल रहे। कलकत्ते के पुलिस विभाग का विज्ञापन कविता में करते हुए वे लिखते हैं-

शरीफों की है जिनके पास दारी
पढ़े-लिखे जो हों हिन्दोस्तानी।
हुनर मन्दों शरीफों खानदानी
पुलिस में नौकरी करना जो चाहें
खुली हैं उनकी बहबूदी की राहें।
हुजूरे हाकिमाने खैरअन्देस
करें वे पेशोपश दरख्वास्त पेश।

यह उल्लेखनीय है कि उन दिनों हिन्दी खड़ी बोली अपना रूप ग्रहण कर रही थी। उसकी शब्द-सम्पदा के मुख्य पांच स्रोत थे-1 संस्कृत, 2 फारसी, 3 लोकभाषाएं, 4 अंग्रेजी, 5 उर्दू-शैली। इसीलिए एक-एक भाव या शब्द के चार-पांच भाषायी रूपान्तर उन दिनों दिखायी दे रहे थे। जैसे-संस्कृत-मूल्य, उर्दू-कीमत, लोक शब्द-दाम, हिन्दी शब्द-भाव, अंग्रेजी शब्द-प्राइस। इसी तरह न्यायालय, अदालत, कचहरी, कोर्ट, अस्पताल, चिकित्सालय, सफाखाना, हॉस्पिटल। तात्पर्य यह है कि अनेक प्रकार के समानार्थक शब्द हिन्दी में चलने शुरू हो गये थे। 'उफुक' ने मुसद्दस और मसनवी में इन शब्दों का मनोवांछित प्रयोग किया है। उर्दू में 'हाली' ने मुसद्दस लिखकर मुस्लिम समाज में जन-जागृति पैदा की थी। उससे प्रेरित होकर गुप्त जी ने *भारत-भारती* (मैथिली शरण गुप्त) लिखी थी। उससे काफी पहले अपने इस अखबार में 'उफुक' ने *आर्यावर्त की तारीखी अजमत* के नाम से 151 बन्द लिखकर मुसद्दस की शैली में भारतीय संस्कृति के पांच हजार वर्षों का जो इतिहास लिखा था, वह सर्वथा सराहनीय है। इस अखबार में उन्होंने

मसनवी विधा के भी कई प्रयोग किए थे। उनकी धार्मिक मसनवी *रामायणः यक काफिया, अवतार, मूर्ति पूजन, तीर्थयात्रा* आदि काफी प्रसिद्ध हैं। इसके चरित्र कदापि कल्पित नहीं हैं। सबके सब पौराणिक ऐतिहासिक पात्र हैं। इसमें क्लासिकल अरबी-फारसी के साथ ही लगभग एक हजार हिन्दी शब्द और मुहावरे भी प्रयुक्त हुए हैं।

अपने अखबार में सम्पादक ने प्रकृति-चित्रण से सम्बन्धित मसनवियां भी पूरी तत्परता के साथ प्रकाशित की। इन्हें हम पद्यबद्ध फीचर या रिपोर्ताज भी कह सकते हैं। इसकी कुछ प्रसिद्ध मसनवियां हैं-'बरसात की बहारें', 'चांद की बहार', 'होली की बहार', 'शाम की बहार', 'बसंत बहार' आदि। ये मसनवियां तिथि-त्योहारों के अनुसार प्रकाशित की गयी हैं।

इस अखबार को लोकप्रिय बनाने के लिए सम्पादक ने प्रेमपरक, युद्ध सम्बन्धी और नीति सम्बन्धी मसनवियां भी कही हैं। उनकी प्रेमकथाओं में 'पद्मावती' और 'नूरजहां' बहुत प्रसिद्ध हुई। 'उफुक' का यह अखबार भारत के महान प्राचीन सांस्कृतिक तथ्यों और उद्धरणों से भरा पड़ा है। वे आर्यावर्त की पुरातन संस्कृति को पुनरुज्जीवित करने और एक प्रगतिवादी राष्ट्र का नव निर्माण करने के लिए कटिबद्ध दिखाई देते हैं। उनका प्रयास रहा है कि यह पद्यबद्ध अखबार जमाने का इतिहास बन जाए। इसका उद्घोष करते हुए वे कहते हैं-

बने बैत अबरूओ चश्में बुता कीं
किया तसनीफ मतला दो जहां का।
बने मिसरा हिलाले आसमां का
नज़ीर उसका नहीं फिक्रे मती में
कलाम उसका है हर बहरो जमीं में।
कुछ इसका ऐसा फैजे इल्मो फन है
रियाजे दहर गुलजारे सफुन है
चकोरें, शायरें शीरीं ज़बां हैं
अनादिल तूति ए हिन्दोस्तां हैं।

कवि का संकल्प है कि एक-एक शेर में दो मिसरे भर जाएं और बिम्बमाला सज जाए। मतले की सफल रचना हो। एक-एक मिसरा आकाश के बालचन्द्र की तरह दिखे। प्रत्येक छन्द अपने कलाम में अनूठा लगे। यह लेखन वक्त के साथ चले और हिन्दुस्तान की बुलबुलों की तरह चहके। 'उफुक' का दावा है कि उनका यह अखबार 'गुलदस्ता कलामे शायरां' है। यह अखबार जरूरत पड़ने पर सारा किस्सा बयां करता है-

मचा दे इफ्तिखारे नज़्म की धूम
दिखा दे जलवए अखबारे मंजूम।
महीने में हो जोशे नज़्म दो बार
बने माह दो हफ्ता जिसमें अखबार।
जहानत कोई बारीकी न छोड़े।
कलम जो हर एक मजमूं में तोड़े।
मिले गाफिल जो महबे खाबिल आराम
तो यह पानी के छींटे का करे काम।
ख़बर के वास्ते यह तार हो जाए
बने यह मुखबिरे हालाते आलम।
रहे पहने यह फिरदौसी का जामा
बयाने जंग में हो शाहनामा।
गरज अखबार के जो जो हैं मन्सब,
वह सब इसमें हों नज़रे अन्सब।

इस नज़्म में अखबार के आदर्शों का एक घोषणा पत्र छपा हुआ है। इसमें लखनऊ केन्द्र की प्रशस्ति की गयी है और अपने युगधर्म से प्रेरित पत्रकारिता की परिकल्पना प्रस्तुत की गयी है।

नज़्म से प्रेरित होकर कई अंग्रेज लेखकों ने शासन का ध्यान इस ओर आकृष्ट किया। अंग्रेजी के प्रसिद्ध वैयाकरण नेसफील्ड ने (जो उन दिनों बस्ती तथा कोटा में नियुक्त थे) इस अखबार के बारे में लिखा–

> Thus he became the proprietor and editor of his renowned *Nazm Akhbar* (from 1888 to 1892, the great part of which was devoted to poetical or versified productions. Even the news items were presented in poetry. A few pages were devoted to prose also. Hazrat Ufuq was his elder brother's right hand in editing the latter's Tamannai Akhbar. He looked to his *Nazm Akhbar* along with *Tamannai Akhbar*.

इस अखबार का सम्पादन करते हुए 'उफुक' निजाम हैदराबाद के उच्च अधिकारी महाराजा गिरिधारी प्रसाद 'बागी' के निमंत्रण पर हैदराबाद आमंत्रित किए गये। 'उफुक' ने वहां आशु रचनाएं कर-करके निजाम को दिखायी, जिससे निजाम ने उनका नागरिक अभिनंदन किया।

'उफुक' की अखबारी कविता पूर्णतः इतिवृत्तात्मक है। उन्होंने समय-समय पर गुलकदई सुखन, मेहरे जराफत आदि की भी रचना की। कविता के साथ-साथ खूबसूरत गद्य लिखने में वे सिद्धहस्त थे। उन्होंने *अरेबियन नाइट्स* का बहुत अच्छा

रूपान्तर किया था। उनकी नाट्य शैली बेताब, आगा हश्र, राधेश्याम, जेबा आदि के समकक्ष थी। कविता में वे ठुमरी, ठप्पा, ध्रुपद की रचना शुद्ध हिन्दी में करते रहे। पहले वे अंग्रेजों के राजभक्त रहे, फिर स्वदेशी से जुड़ गये। लेखन में अपना सर्वस्व निछावर कर देने के कारण उनका पारिवारिक जीवन आर्थिक दृष्टि से अस्त-व्यस्त रहा। आजीवन संघर्षरत रहने के कारण 12 सितम्बर 1913 को 49 वर्ष की अवस्था में उनकी मृत्यु हो गयी।

अपने इस अखबार द्वारा उन्होंने लखनऊ के *अवध पंच* को शिकस्त दी, जो सज्जाद हुसैन जैसे हास्य-व्यंग्य के महारथी रचनाकार द्वारा सम्पादित लखनऊ का लोकप्रिय पत्र था। 'उफुक' का मत था "इस अखबार में पूरे दयार के वाकियात इस तरह बयान हों, गोया कि वह आंखों देखे हों। यानी अखबार जामेजम या जमशेद के उस प्याले की तरह होगा, जिसमें सब कुछ दिखायी देता था। अखबार रिआया गमख्वार होगा। उसके जरिये किसी को परेशान नहीं किया जाएगा। हस्बे जरूरत वाकियात और तन्कीद ज़राफर्त में बयान होंगे, जिसका अपना अलग ही अंदाज होगा। ज़मीमा (परिशिष्ट) में जो बहारेनस्र (गद्य) दिखलायेंगे, वह खूबसूरत नए फूलों की तरह खुशनुमा होगी। अखबार के सारे लवाजिमात (उद्योग) दिलकश अंदाज में बरते जायेंगे।

इस अखबार की तारीफ में देशभर के पत्रकारों ने अपनी प्रतिक्रियायें प्रकट की थी। *आगरा अखबार* ने लिखा था-

नज़्म अखबार किस अन्दाज़ से निकला देखो।
अब तलक हिन्द में जो तुमने न देखा, देखो।
है तमन्ना व उफुक ज़मज़मा पैरा इसके
ऐसा अखबार न देखा न सुने ये नग़मे।

'उफुक' ने बर्तानिया सरकार की आर्थिक नीति, साम्प्रदायिक दृष्टि और टैक्स वसूली पर पुरजोर प्रहार किया। एक अंक में वे लिखते हैं-

टकस हिन्दोस्तां के वास्ते भूखी भवानी है
कमाई सबकी चट करने को मेदा कर्बसानी है।
बलाए आसमानी है, बलाए आसमानी है।
यह वह गोला है जो लगता है इंसानों के सीने पर
यह वह जोंक है जिसको है महारत खून पीने पर।
यह वह सांप जो बैठा है लोगों के खजानों पर
यह वह घुन है जो खा जाता गल्लों को दुकानों पर
यह दौलत लूटने के वास्ते है नादिरे सानी

शाहे महमूद गजनी है यह अहमदशाह दुर्रानी।
निहत्था होके लूटे काफिला जो ये वो डाकू है
रिआया को ये जीता निगल जाता, ये हलाकू है।

नज़्म अखबार में लिखी गयी खबरों का अंदाज़ गज़लगोई का होता था। 5 मार्च 1890 में शाह ईरान हिन्दुस्तान आये, उस पर यह अखबार लिखता है-

ज़रा ऐ हिन्द तू होशियार हो जा।
टक्स के वास्ते तैयार हो जा।
लगा दे घर में फिर सर्राफ के आग
लंगोटी में जरा फिर खेल ले फाग।

इसी प्रकार एक अंक में 'दिल्ली दरबार' *की जो भर्त्सना की गयी है, वह भी* स्मरणीय है। सर्वाधिक विस्मय कारक बात यह है कि 12 पृष्ठों का यह अखबार अधिकतर 'उफुक' साहब का ही लिखा हुआ होता था। हां, बीच-बीच में कुछ आलेख फरहत, तमन्ना, नैसां, ज़र्रा, मौलाना सफीक, ज्वाला प्रसाद 'बर्क', बालकृष्ण 'कमर', आदि के भी दिखायी देते हैं। इस समूचे अखबार में समकालीन पत्र-पत्रिकाओं की तरह अलग-अलग स्तम्भ नहीं थे। इसमें सम्पादक पूरे पखवारे की महत्वपूर्ण घटनाएं चुन लेता था और उनका विवरण देता हुआ, साथ ही अपनी टिप्पणी देता हुआ, उन्हें क्रमशः प्रस्तुत करता जाता था। घटनाओं का चयन सोद्देश्य हुआ करता था। सम्पादक की दृष्टि प्रायः संवेदनशील हादसों पर रहती थी। इसमें प्रकाशित समाचारों को पढ़ने से प्रतीत होता है कि मध्यवर्गीय प्रबुद्ध नागरिकों में अंग्रेजों की दासता से मुक्त होने की अकुलाहट व्यक्त होने लगी थी, किन्तु उनके आगे कोई निश्चित दिशा-दृष्टि नहीं थी।

इस प्रकार *नज़्म* अखबार कवित्वपूर्ण पत्रकारिता का एक 'न भूतो न भविष्यति' अपवाद बनकर प्रकट हुआ। इसने कविता को अखबारी शिल्प से जोड़ा। अखबार को जनजागरण की ओर मोड़ा और पैन फारसी को हिन्दुस्तानी की तरह तोड़ा। इसकी कुछ प्रतियां सालारजंग म्यूजियम हैदराबाद में सुरक्षित हैं। आवश्यकता सभी अवशेषों को पुरातात्विक अस्तित्व प्रदान करने की है। इसलिए कि यह छंद बद्ध कविता में पत्रकारिता का एक विरल एवं विलक्षण प्रयोग है।

Section II

Print Media, Visual and Performing Arts

13

Folk Songs – An Effective Means of Communication*

(Special Reference to U.P. Tradition)

Nishi Misra

In India rural society had given birth to folk culture, religion, music and dance tradition, so also it had made use of folk songs as the most effective and handy means of communication. It still remains effective means of communication because of its musical quality and its social and religiocultural content. Oral Tradition has never ceased to exist and it still continues to remain an effective means of communication even after the invention of writing technique as a more durable means of communication. This has been more true in the case of rural northern India, where illiteracy continues to remain a dominant feature of the rural society. Innate conservatism, deep religiosity and relatively slow degree of modernization have been additional factors which have contributed to the continuity of folk culture, religion, dance and music tradition in India as an effective means of dialogue between the past and the future through the present time.

Until a little more than half a century back, folk cultural traditions, music and lyrics were excluded from the area of historical studies in India because of peoples' natural aversion to acceptance of new ideas and concepts. That is why study of Oral Tradition remained limited within the confines of American sociological and social anthropological studies largely being centred on Latin American and African social studies. Luckily, things have started moving in the right direction, and Oral Tradition is now being given its rightful place among sources of social history of India.

Coming back to the folk song tradition. We can point it out here that folk music and songs have continued to have their relevance much because of their happy blending of socio-economic and cultural occasions with religiosity and also with rhythmical structure of songs. Such occasions have been providing the growing up girls in general and newly married daughters-in-law in particular occasion like in-house training (by way of their ceremonial welcome leading to their acceptance in the family of new in-laws.)

Such social occasions have also been providing platform for communication of new ideas and information, as well as, social connectivity among people of different generations. So also, folk songs and music occasionally find relatively larger audience if they happen to be organized in temple premises or some common open space, such as, panchayat land or open areas not far from their fields. They also offer opportunities of commingling of the people belonging to various social groups and, as such, they continue to maintain their egalitarian character.

Folk music and folk songs continue to add meaning, colour and hope to otherwise harsh reality of dull and monotonous rural life based on agriculture and related activities. Folk music and folk songs boost the morale of the hard working peasantry and they had gaiety to the general atmosphere.

Folk songs have made their happy blending with rural activities, such as, ploughing and preparation of field during sowing season, harvesting of ripened crop, extraction of sugarcane juice for making of *gur*, pounding of wheat, etc. into flour, extraction of oil in oil press (*Kolhu*) by mongers. Pre-sowing and post harvest occasions are still treated as occasions which call for festive gatherings and singing of songs and music. So also, child birth, religious ceremonies like, *mundan* (tonsure), *janau* (thread ceremony), son's marriage, daughter's marriage, pre-and post-marriage celebrations, departure of newly married daughter (*bidai*), arrival of new daughter-in-law (*agwani*), are occasions of social gathering and feasting. They are considered as most suitable time and occasion for giving thanks to divinities (Mother Goddess, etc.) for ensuring the possibility of trouble-free occasions.

The following songs throw welcome light on social and religious folk songs prevalent in the Gangetic doab:

1. "Birds are chirping with the dawn and farmers with turbans on their heads and picks on their shoulder are going to the field".[1]
2. However, the young farmer requests his beautiful wife to visit him in the field under the pretext of bringing him food.[2]
3. The tradition of singing lyrics on the occasion of birth of the child is linked with the tradition of songs dedicated to Kṛishṇa's birth.[3]
4. But, such happy occasions were occasionally associated with killing of animals for preparation of curry for the grand feast, is indicated by a folk song dedicated to Rāma's birthday. This also, in a way, is indicative of a plea made in favour of protection of wild life.[4]
5. Parents and brothers of lady of the house and also of the daughter-in-law traditionally sent yellow sarees and ornaments to them on ceremonial occasions.[5]
6. Like the *mundan* ceremony, thread ceremony was considered as a holy act among the upper caste people.[6]
7. Some folk songs speak of parrot, etc. being charged with the duty of locating a suitable match for a growing up daughter.[7]
8. Among the Gangetic doab people, some sort of protest by mother of the son getting married and noble promises by the latter to keep on respecting her interest happens to be the subject matter of a folk song.[8]
9. The welcome of bride and bridegroom in parental house happens to be the theme yet another song.[9]
10. A folk song underlines the difference of position of boy's father vis-à-vis that of girl's father.[10]
11. The grand feast on the occasion Rāma's marriage is remembered again and again in a folk song.[11]
12. The daughter married off in a distant village narrates her feeling in a song.[12]
13. *Bhajans* or songs sung in prays of gods/goddesses, etc. too had their distinct flavour.[13]

INDIAN CINEMA AND FOLK SONG

The middle of the 20th century saw a large number of folk songs being borrowed by the Hindi Cinema musicians and choreographers in films like Kalapani, Bandini,[14] etc. which indicate popularity of those songs in the cinema world. A yet another case of such large scale borrowing of folk music and folk songs can be seen in films Tisri Kasam.

NOTES AND REFERENCES

* All life forms – whether we can or cannot see them – have, through the evolutionary process, learnt to express their presence, at least to members of their own species (in matters of hunger and biological needs) and also to word off members of other clans and species from their sanctified territories, by sending their standardized signals as the earliest means of communication.

This has been true of all species before the birth of mammals who began using different types of standardized sounds with the same objective. The Great Ape, added a yet another dimension to the till then in use means of communication by using hand and facial gestures. This made their communication techniques more effective. Hominid predecessors of the modern Intelligent Man too used the same methods of communication because of their inability to invent language.

Only the Intelligent Man was successful in breaking the sound barrier because of his success in inventing and successfully using the language in its true word-meaning context. All this took a very long time (between one lakh years and twenty thousand years ago).

Man's capacity to speak and tell, see and learn and teach and train his succeeding generations, immensely contributed to the dawn of Neolithic Revolution and birth of rural societies, sometime between seven – six thousand years before now. (R.V.)

1. भिनुसारे चिरैया बोलन लागीं,
   पूरब माँ छाई उषा की लाली, बगियन माँ कलियाँ खिलन लागीं।
   सिर वा पगड़िया बंधिले कांधे पे कुदलिया लेहिले,
   आगे-आगे हल चले, पाछे से किसनवां, खेतवा जा ला हो सँवरिया।।
2. मीठी तोहरी बोलिया गोरी, चाल चलेलु अलबेली।
   चढ़ति दुपहरिया माँ लाई जलपनवा, टक-टक ताकेला बेइमनवा।।
3. जेहि दिन कान्ह जन्म लीन्हें नौबति बाजइ हो,
   एहो, उपजे हैं दीन दयाल दुनहऊं कुलतारन हो।

कपिलन्ह दूध दुहैंहौं मैं कान्ह अन्हवइहौं रे,
रेसम धरिया ओढ़ैहौं, पलंग पउढ़इहौं रे।।
लाल के बड़े बड़े बैन कांजरु भल सोहंइ हो,
अब ऑंजे है फूफू सुभद्रा, उँगरि नहिं डोलइ रे।

4. छापक पेड़ छिउलिया तो पतवन गहबर हो,
एहो, तेहि तर ठाढ़ी हरिनियां, तौ मन अति अनमनि हो।
मचियई बैठी कौसल्या तो हरिनी अरज करै हो,
रानी मंसवा तो सीझहि रोसइया, खलरिया हमें देतिऊ हो।
जाहु हरिनि घर अपने, खलरिया नहिं देबेऊ हो,
हरिनि खलरी की खँजरी मढ़उबे तो राम मोरे खेलहई हो।
जब जब बाजे खंजरिया सबद सुनि अनकई हो,
हरिनी ठाढ़ी ढकोलिया के नीचे हरिन का बिसूरई हो।

5. अरी-अरी कारी कोयलिया आंगन मोरे बइठउहो,
कोइलरि आजु मोरे पहिलु बियाहु, नेवत दइ आवऊ हो।
अरी-अरी बाबा केरी चेरिया से हमरी लड़ैतिनि हो,
चेरिया देखि आवो भैया कै नगरिया, वीरन नहीं आए हो।
ओगे-आगे आवै छिया गागर, चुनरी गहबर हो,
एहों लिल्ले घोड़े भैया असवार तो डोलिया भावजरानी हो।
एक साध जिय उपजी सबहिं विधि पुरवऊ हो,
राजा हमरे नैहर लगे जाओ, पियरि लइ आवौ रे।
तुम्हरो तो नैहर दूरी बसे, कोसवन को चले,
धना घरहीं माँ पियरी रंगाओ चौक लै पहिरऊ हो।
पियरी तो हमरी सगुन केरी, पहिलि चौक मोरी,
राजा हमरे नैहर तुम जाओ, पियरि लइ आवौ रे।

6. नदिया किनारे बर पीपर, बरुआ पुकारै हो,
पठै दे बाबा मोरे नाव, बरुआ चले आवइं हो।
ना मोरे नाव नवइया, न दुसरो खिवैया रे,
जेहि का जनए केरी साध, बरुआ चढ़ि आवइ हो।

7. सावन सुवना मै घिऊ - गुर पालेऊँ चैत चना की दाल रे,
अब सुवना तुम भयउ सजुगवा, बेटी कै बर हेरै जायो रे।
उड़त उड़त तुम जायो रे सुगनवा बैठेऊ डरिया ओनायरे,
डरिया ओनाय बैठि पखना फुलायो, चितवयो नज़र घुमाय रे।
जे बर सुगना तुम देखेऊ सुंदर जेकरी चाल गंभीर रे,
जेहि घर सुगना सम्पति देखेऊ तेही घर रचेउ बियाहु रे।

8. तू त चलेऊ पूता गोरी बियाहन,
दुधवा का मोल किहे जायो रे।

सरग तोरइया मइया कब लौ,
दुधवा का मोल कैसे होय रे।
गोरी बियाहि जब लौटब मइया मोरी,
इतना वचन सुनि लेहु रे।
हमहूँ जो होइबे बाबा के सेवकिया,
मोरी धना दासी तोहार रे।

9. बाजन-बाजे दुआर रंगीला दुल्हा ब्याहन आया,
मंगल कलश धरे है गुजरिया, चौमुख दियना बार रंगीला।
हरे-हरे गोबरइ चौकि पुरी है, पुरवइ सोहगिले नार,
समधी जी ठाढ़े आगे दुअरवा हाथ फूलन केरा हार।

10. सॅकरा है समधी तुम्हरो दुअरवा, सॉकर है दरवाज रे।
कहो तो समधी दुआरे पे उतरी, कहो बगीचै जाई रे।।
काहे का समधी दुआरे पै उतरो, काहे बगीचई जाओ रे।
लीपी औ पोती है यह चौबरिया बइठउ फैलि - बिछाय रे।।
समधी जी बइठे अलीचा गलीचा, श्रीवर फैल बिछाय रे।
मोरे स्वामी बइठे हैं कुश की संथरिया अंग छिलि छिलि जाई रे।।
बेटी के माया सूरज मनावे, धिया उपजइ नहीं कोख रे।।
बेटी के बाबा सूरज मनावै धिया उपजई दुइ चार रे।
समधी दमाद दुन्हउॅ दल उमड़े धनि-धनि भाग हमारि रे।।

11. राम लखन जब जेंवन बइठे, देत सखी सब गारी जी।
गोरे दसरथ, गोरी कौसल्या, गोरे सब सरदारी जी।।
लक्ष्मण, भरत कौसल्या गोरी, तुम्हरी सूरत क्यों कारी जी।
एक बात का बुरा ना मान्यो, कहियत सुनी सुनाई जी।।
ऋषियन के संग जाय सिधारीं बहिनी बुआ तुम्हारी जी।

12. काहे को ब्याही विदेस रे, लखिया बाबुल मोरे।
हम तो बाबुल तोरे अंगना की चिड़ियां, भोर भए उड़ि जांय।।
बेटे को दीन्हों महल दुमहला हमको दियो परदेस रे।
भइया के रोइबे से छतिया फटत है, भाभी खड़ी मुसकाय रे।।
मैया कहे बेटी नित उठि अइयो, बाबा कहै छठ मास रे।
भैया कहें बहिनी काजे औ कामे, भउजी कहैं का काम रे।।

13. रहना नहीं देस बिराना है,
यह संसार कगद की पुड़िया, बूंद परे गल जाना है।
अल्लाह मेरे आवेंगे, मोहम्मद ऑवेंगे।
आगे गंगा थम ली, जमुना हिलोरें लेय।।
बीच खडी बीबी फातिमा, उम्मत बलैयां ले।
मालिनि गूंथे सेहरा, दूल्हा बने रसूल।।

14. 1. नज़र लागी राज तोरे बंगले पर,
जो मै होती राजा कारी वदरिया, बरस रहती राजा तोरे बंगले पर।
जो मैं होती राजा बेला चमेलिया, गमक रहती राजा तोरे बंगले पर।।

14. 2. ढूँढो–ढूँढो रे साजना ढूँढो रे मोरे कान का बाला।
मोरा बाला चन्दा का जैसे हाला रे,
जामे लाले लाले मोतियन की लटके माला।।

14. 3. झूठ बोले कौव्वा काटे, काले कौए से डरियो।
मैं माइके चली जाउँगी तुम देखते रहियो।।
तू मायके चली जाएगी मैं डंडा लेकर आऊंगा।
तू डंडा लेकर आएगा मैं पेड़ पर चढ़ जाऊंगी।।

14. 4. दीदी तेरा देवर दीवाना, हाय राम चिड़ियों को डाले दाना।

14

Role of Theatre in Communication

Kavita Nagpal

Communication in theatre is a complex construct of social and structural modes involving millennia of interaction between spirit and convention. Traditions of performing art forms- dance, theatre, music – their social function, communication patterns can be deliberated in the context of their evolution in the crucible of time and space. Theatre is the most complete art form because it incorporates all spatial and temporal dimensions, literature, visual art, music, movement/dance and uses the human being as the primary instrument of expression in the completeness of body, spirit, mind, emotions and imagination.

A unique feature of the dramatic art is its social orientation. It is an art form which fulfils its functional purpose through social organization of live happenings communicated socially. For a theatre event to take place two groups of participants are required, the performers and the spectators. It is only through the interaction of these two sets that theatre occurs. The actor cannot replicate a moment passed on stage. Each time a theatre act is staged, the energy transmitted is different. And the transmission and reception of this energy has as much to do with the performance as with the compositions of the two groups – the performers and spectators.

It also has to do with time and issue/issues at that point of time in the life of a society, and how well it is prepared to tackle those issues. In order to have comprehensive view of contemporary Indian theatre it is essential not only to follow the direction of its development, its links with historic tradition, societal change, but also take into account the several theories propounded on drama over the millennia. According to ancient Indian tracts on drama, there is an ideal moment of communication. The moment of pure joy occurs when the spectator and the performer become one single entity and share the same sensibility as 'sahridaya'. For this wondrous conjuration, not only must the actors be gifted with emotional maturity and aesthetic sensitivity, but so too the audience. The equal participation of the spectator for a complete realization of theatre experience is a unique aspect of the 'Rasa' theory as enshrined in the *Nāṭyaśāstra*.

The *Nāṭyaśāstra* (NS) is one of the most ancient and certainly the most comprehensive treatises on dramaturgy. Its authorship is ascribed to Muni/sage Bharata (2nd Century BC- 2nd Century AD). It is said that God Brahmā created drama and then asked Bharata to simplify it for practical purposes. The story as narrated in the NS goes thus: The gods went to Brahmā with a complaint: "People all over the world have taken to vulgar ways; they have grown greedy, avaricious, jealous and quarrelsome; they do not know whether they are happy or miserable. Please give us some diversion (toy) that can both be heard and seen. The Sudras cannot have access to the Vedic works, therefore create a fifth Veda that can be accessible to all castes."[1]

Taking elements from the four Vedas; word from *Ṛigveda*, music, chanting and rhythmic flow of speech and sound from *Sāmaveda*, from *Yajurveda* gesture, the use of body and its accompanying ritualistic and symbolic functions, from *Atharvaveda* emotional acting that illuminates the 'Rasa' theory – Bharata create the fifth Veda, the *Nāṭyaśāstra*.[2] It is indeed ironic that that a text accessible to the Sudras should be called a Veda. Reading between the lines and informed by its presence today, it is almost certain that there existed some theatre catering to the uninhibited tastes of the audience whom Bharata calls Sudra. And this theatre was obviously not acceptable to the ruling classes.

The fact that Sanskrit dramatists like Bhāsa, Śūdraka and others used both the court language Sanskrit and the people's language Prakrit indicates their desire to communicate with an audience beyond the court to the larger public.[3]

The world created by the performers on stage is 'theatre' as distinct from 'drama' the written text. Theatre can exist without words, on mime, music, movements, sound alone, (dance drama, ballet, modern dance, mime shows, etc.) but conventionally it is built up from a pre-given text that is the artist's creative impression of images of the perceived external world. This eclectic choice of a human situation/condition being is determined by the writer's world-view and is a fictional account of reality.

The transformation of drama into theatre occurs with the mediation of the director, actors and spectators. Drama, like fiction, tells a story. However, instead of relying only on language or pictures, the story is narrated by actors by subtle art of voice, facial expression, and gestures try and bring the story physically alive. Acting, as the word implies, is the closest art to living action. The art removes the actual consequences from the spectator's life and people can vicariously (and more vividly than with literature) experience many things they may not, would not, should not, want to have in real life.

Drama is essentially the demonstration of a situation, a theme, an idea, a suggestion or possibility. Plot, character, theme, mood and language are important, but these only serve the total aural/visual effect. Theatre is a group art on both sides of the spotlights, and hence offers several person-to-person, group to person, person to aspects of production, etc. having possibilities of communication. It acquires other dimensions when the group is not separated by a spotlight and occupies a shared space, like in Badal Sircar's theatre where actors are in touching distance, or in street theatre, or traditional secular theatre like Therrukothu of Andhra Pradesh, Swang of Himachal Pradesh, etc.

Besides communicating with the spectator, the actors have to communicate with each other and with the animate and inanimate objects in the performing space. Each actor has his/her built character – after long interaction with the director, the text and with himself/herself as a social being. This experience is brought into action during the interface with other actors, stage objects and the audience responses in time and space. All these communication processes are vibrantly active during a performance. These factors influence the interactive show as actors are constantly discovering new points of interaction- hence the 'newness' in each performance.

What is the role of theatre in communication? In ancient Greece, drama was divided into tragedy and comedy and masks with corner of the mouth turned up or down indicating the genre were used to assure the audience of the type of drama on offer. The purpose of dramatic art is to entertain and enlighten at the same time. Tragedy holds our interest with its dread, apprehension, deep probing of emotion and thought as the consequences of actions and character traits are revealed. In comedy certain actions, sights and perspectives may suddenly release psychological tensions and make us laugh. Through observation of folly we may become wiser. The genres have however become mixed with several variations like farce, satire, tragicomedy, melodrama, mystery, horror and avantgarde experiments that do not strictly comply with classical traditions, communication has become more intricate.

In his daily life an individual dwells in a situation of social engagements that involve him directly or in mediated contact with other people. Through verbal and nonverbal acts he expresses his opinion on the situation, his actual participation and himself. Linguistic signals are obvious but participants in conversation can also draw inferences about each other's individual characteristics through appearance and map a fairly accurate chart of the inner social and psychological set up during the interaction. That is a certain degree of knowledge gathered from sources other than words – tonal quality, gestures, expressions, body tension, employed as signs and symbols for communication.

The form and content of communication varies. It may be personal as in a conversation – though this interaction is also a social exchange. The encounter may be between an individual and an artistic creation – reading, viewing a painting, listening to music, etc. Or it may be between a group of people and an artwork or performance. Or there may be a complex interaction between individuals two distinct groups where both may be active as in a game of skills or one physically inert as in a theatre.

The degree, nature, purpose and function of communication may differ, but the source of its manifestations abstract form reality. The signs and symbols used attempt the creation of an image of the perceived external world. The process involves a human transformation of nature where the artist sensorily and intellectually explores the possibilities in a selected situation and presents an individual image. When communicated this artistic image evokes an emotional reaction that reaches out to other images and phenomena giving the particular object a generalized meaning. The artist's reflection of essential reality in a specific state is grasped and interpreted by the receiver according to his understanding of the phenomenon. Thus we have a movement from the general to the specific and to a changed general.

For instance, in theatre, an actor takes an object construct, a work of art abstracted from real life and transforms it. The end product is not real but an artistic representation (of another artistic representation), which has a life of its own. This, then, is communicated to the spectator/audience who will relate it to own life as it is concretely lived. There is a living contact between two groups of people, performers and audience in relation to spatial constructs divined out of animate and inanimate objects in time and space. Each aspect of a performance in its signified state possesses dynamic possibilities and ergo its communication.

Cultural variations affect communication as much as the degree of theatre consciousness does. An audience may be tense or restless, offensive or defensive, it may react sharply or foolishly or not at all. In each case the nature of the performance will alter. The player may try and woo the spectator, or assault his senses. Depending on the nature of the interaction, he may love, caress, shock or try and appease the viewer. I remember vividly a performance in which I had to deliver a long emotional soliloquy. The play was Kannad writer Adhya Rangacharya's 'Suno Janmejay'(a contemporary interpretation of the myth in which the Sutradhara was introduced in modern theatre for the first time) And the audience at one end began to twitter. I then directed my entire emotional force in that direction and was soon blessed with silent attention.

The electronic media has to a large extent eroded the role of theatre as communicator. It is so much simpler to switch on the TV slide in a DVD and watch a whole saga of human emotions spawned and bred in the artificial confines of studios painted and plastered over by glitz and gum, edited and spliced to increase cinematic value, in the confines of a home than to venture out to see theatre. The function of light entertainment is easily served. It requires little mind and small heart to passively receive flickering signals in a time where attention spans have been reduced to seconds.

There was a time when the role of theatre had an important role to play in a community. People collected in street corners, in mohalla courtyards, in temples to witness live performances. These performances of legends and myths were inevitably ruled by the needs and aspirations of the people and changed form and content with time. These shows entertained as they helped sort out issues and offer succour. The Sūtradhāra, or traditional holder of strings in a play, is conventionally allowed to comment on current affairs, recast dialogue to focus on issues of social import, and assume the role of a bridge between society and drama. Certain forms and conventions are conducive to cognition because they have evolved as cultural traditions. Musical folk forms like Nautanki of U.P., Bhawai of Gujarat, Khayal of Rajasthan and a myriad other traditional modes of enactment like the Ramlila and the Raslila, are endemic to a region and suitable mediums of communication.

Conventions rise out of forms of social consciousness. Man, when faced by a problematic situation tries to resolve it and give it coherent structure. This structure is the outcome of his social experience and worldview. This understanding, when it strikes a similar chord in society makes the given structure a reference point for apprehension of similar phenomenon. Such reference points then form sets of conventions. Crystallized social experience is the content of tradition. Tradition thus having birth in social consciousness can only be activated when experience is unfrozen and allowed to interact with new emerging experience.

The musical Nautanki and the declamatory prose and verse style of Parsi theatre (inspired by Victorian drama) have long been part of the theatre tradition of the Hindustani-speaking belt. In his play 'Bakri', renowned Hindi writer, Sarveshwar Dayal Saxena, draws upon traditional elements from these forms, popular folk music and realistic drama to create theatre symbols at once modern and endemic to the region. This play, which I directed, deals with a *Bakri* (Goat) and exploitation of the peasants at the hands of the capitalist in connivance with a politician and religious leader was played in different social milieus – on Chandni Chowk streets, at factory gates, for students, blue and white collar workers, etc.

The peasant, controlled by the logic of belief is moved to acceptance of the enshrinement of the *Bakri*. The appeals of the woman who cries out against the injustice of installing her *Bakri* in a temple as the descendant of Mahatma Gandhi's goat, and thus depriving her of her sole livelihood initially go unheard. The intervention of and interaction with a Youth militant peasant-worker provokes spontaneous applause; an unconscious realization of the issue of exploitation. This feeling of resentment is given voice when at a given moment of emotional stress a unified opposition, led by the Youth, confronts the exploiters. This class confrontation is designed to indicate the historical outcome of such social conflicts and provoke the audience to apprehend not only individual struggles against oppression, but also to enlarge the scope and relate the specific to the general.

The function and role of theatre is to communicate the present truth with a view to improving the quality of life through heightened awareness. Each character has to be honed in such a manner that she/he can invest the 'type' (policeman, political leader, capitalist, religious man, etc.) with individual features in a manner so as to convey the typical immediately and show the relationship between an isolated phenomenon and its general occurrence. The causal relationship between external and internal action has to be so evolved that the link between the abstract idea and concrete expression is maintained at a degree of intimacy and yet not be so obvious. For instance when staging a play about say eunuchs or *hijras*, it is as important to show their lifestyle and how and why *hijras* are social outcastes as to show their inner life, their outer actions must indicate the inner reality. Communication is a mixture of direct experience and symbolic meaning, some of which may refer to facts conceptually and some of which is interpretative opinion.

Communication involves a conscious freedom of choice. The choice of one means the rejection of the other. It also implies the choice of values and the relativity of good and bad. As human beings our essence is divine and positive, but our life brings us in confrontation with its relative opposites. Our essence motivates us to choose the beautiful over the ugly, good over bad, true over false; in communication it prompts us to choose honesty over dishonesty. Universal truth in any artistic communication occurs when the artist by speaking for himself speaks for other people, when his creation gives people their voice and possible directions in mastering their own environment for understanding action: A genuine artist can never create for 'himself' alone.

In theatre it is the audience that decides if the communication process has succeeded. The role of theatre is to make the art universal by providing a wide range of emotional cognition, to reveal advancing and progressive trends in society, so that the spectator has maximum freedom to reach out for the human ideal, the essence. Communication in art however cannot take place if this freedom, truth and universality functions outside the laws of art. Theatre must be an aesthetic value to fill its role as a communicator of its world of ideas.

As Peter Brook, the international Theatre Guru puts it,

> Theatre only exists at the precise moment when these two worlds – that of the actor and that of the audience – meet: a society in miniature, a microcosm brought together every evening within a space. Theatre's role is to give this microcosm a burning, fleeting taste of another world, in which our present world is integrated and transformed (*The Shifting Point*, published by Random House).

NOTES AND REFERENCES

1. *Bharatanāṭyaśāstra*, Vol. II, chap. 1. 9-12 (ed.) N.P. Unni, Delhi 1998.
   ग्राम्य धर्मप्रवृत्ते तु कामलोभवशं गते।
   ईष्याक्रोधादिसम्मूढे लोके सुखितदु:खिते।।
   ....
   महेन्द्रप्रमुखैर्देवैरुक्त: किल पितामह:।
   क्रीडनीयकमिच्छामो दृश्यं श्राव्यं च यद् भवेत्
   न वेदव्यवहारोऽयंसंश्राव्य: शूद्रजातिषु।
   तस्मात् सृजापरं वेदं पञ्चमं सार्ववर्णिकम्।।
2. Ibid., chap. 1.1718
   जग्राह पाठ्यमृग्वेदात् सामभ्यो गीतमेवच
   यजुर्वेदादभिनयान् रसानाथर्वणादपि
   वेदोपवेदै: संबद्धो नाट्यवेदो महात्मना।
   एवं भगवता सृष्टो ब्रह्मणा सर्ववेदिना।।
3. Although one cannot refute this statement, we have to keep in mind the Sanskrit drama tradition which insisted upon the use of the Sanskrit language by brāhmaṇas and other upper caste people and the usage of the Prakrit language by women and low caste people. The only exception of this rule happened to be the court jester (*vidūshaka*) who used the Prakrit language in spite of being a brāhmaṇa. That is, Sanskrit and Prakrit languages were used simultaneously. The mixed audience present there was supposed to be understanding the dialogues. Otherwise, the folk drama and theatre could hardly have any relevance. Even the *Nāṭyaśāstra vol.3,* chap., 18.34-35, 40-41 make reference to Sanskrit as the language of upper caste and class people. However, Prakrit was to be used by others (ibid., chap. 18, 37-39.) (R.V.)

15

Some Stalwarts of Indian Music

K.P. Srivastava

Perhaps memories fade with age and time. But if one concentrates and thinks about them they come rushing to mind though not in any order.

My interest in music and dance began when I was in my teens. Sometime after a brief period of imprisonment during the 'Quit India' movement of 1942, I joined the Bhatkhande School of Music in Lucknow as a student of vocal music. Soon after I gravitated to Kathak. M.S. Kalyanpurkar was the dance teacher. A year or so later I became a disciple of the renowned Guru Shambhu Maharaj, whose nephew, Birju Maharaj, and sons Ram Mohan and Krishna Mohan are now making waves.

For sometime I toyed with the idea of making a career in performing arts, but that was not to be. The pressure of family, college and university also contributed to it. Somehow, I entered journalism a little before Independence in 1947. But my interest in music and dance has not waned even today though there are fewer occasions to renew contacts or even attend performances by noted artistes. Over the years, I think, I developed an ear for music and an eye for dance and had the privilege of attending performances of some of the top notchers and even knowing them personally and learning some finer points of their art.

Many, Hindus and Muslims, regard music and dance as service to the Divine Being and as a means of peace to one's mind and soul. *Sāmaveda* and Bharata's *Nāṭyaśāstra* are known to be the earliest texts which have inspired many an early practioner of the two arts. Compositions of Amir Khusro, known as 'Tooti-i-Hind' and a disciple of Hazrat Nizamuddin Aulia, and many others are an eternal evidence of it. *'Chhap tilak sab chhini mo se naina milae ke,'* the opening line of one of his famous compositions, so often sung by qawwals at dargahs and gatherings of music lovers, is an instance. Some danseuse call their art as 'dreaming with the feet'. Dance performances, whichever school they might belong to, invariably begin with an invocation to God. Themes of most Kathak performances are woven round Rādhā and Kṛishṇa. Times have brought many an innovation in the discipline of dance. Now we see ballets in Kathak and Bharata Nāṭyam which were earlier witnessed in Europe only. I first enjoyed it in Moscow in the fifties in the famous Bolshoi theatre. Many would remember Anna Pavalova, who after shifting to London, joined Uday Shankar and graduated to becoming his dance partner.

In U.P. of those days Lucknow, Allahabad and Banaras were the centres of performing arts with some well known *gurus,* functions used to be organized at regular intervals and many an artiste would participate in them. I used to attend as many as I could and never had to buy a ticket courtesy friends.

I considered myself close to Shambhu Maharaj and used to accompany him to *'mujras'* – quite a respectable word then – in and outside the city. He joined my marriage party to Hardoi in 1948 and it was something like a surprise to most. He was bestowed with titles like king of Kathak, *Nritya Samrat* and was peerless in *bhava,* i.e. demonstrating lyrics through facial expressions and gestures. When in a mood he could spend the whole night in interpreting just two or four lines of a *thumri* or *dadra* or an Urdu couplet.

Once Maharaj was obsessed with the idea of expressing *Ghazals* through *bhava*. His favourite couplet *'Hai woh waqt-e-naza aur unka tasalli dena/Mera ro ke ye kahna ki meri yaad rahe'* which he interpreted through *bhava* became so popular that there used to be vociferous demand for repeat performance.

Yet another was the interpretation though *bhava* the difference between *tuu na jaa, tum na jao,* and *aap na jayen*. He used to preface it by saying Rādhārani is entreating Sri Kṛishṇa not to leave for Mathura.

Those conversant with Urdu or Hindustani well know the difference. But to express it through facial expression and hand gestures is quite a different thing.

After abolition of zamindari in UP, patrons of performing arts dwindled. Those who were making a living out of it and training a new generation found it difficult. Some of Shambhu Maharaj's friends and well-wishers approached the then secretary of the Sangeet Natak Academy for help. She was willing but for that Maharaj would have to shift to Delhi. It was really a Herculean job. Leaving Lucknow and taking up a job was unthinkable for him. Ultimately he agreed and came to Delhi in mid-fifties where he died of throat cancer in the sixties.

Citizens of Lucknow have installed his bust in the famous Aminabad Park.

Uday Shankar earned a name in Europe. Anna Pavalova, the leading Russian ballerina, who was then based in London, was attracted to Kathak and trained under him for sometime. I am told she was his dance partner for some time. Later Ms. Simki, a Swiss heiress, took interest in him and his troupe and for a time was his dance partner too. With Simki he came to India in 1942 and was billed for a show in a posh cinema hall in the upmarket Hazratganj (Lucknow). Shankar had invited Maharaj with some of his friends. Professionally Maharaj's status was higher than that of Shankar as the former belonged to a Gharana, unlike Shankar. Maharaj later invited the troupe to dinner at his Jhaulal ka pul residence where a room was kept ready for such occasions. It was a sit-on-the-floor dinner. We were in attendance.

It was at this show that I first saw Ustad Alauddin Khan conducting his orchestra. Baba, as he was known, handed over the baton to Timir Baran and sometime later settled down in Maihar. He was a devotee of a goddess on a hill near his residence.

Baba was a sarodiya but could play on sixty instruments, it is said. Nal Tarang, made out of gun barrels, is his invention. He often broke out into singing while playing the sarod apparently for the benefit of his audience. I have a tape of one such performance.

There used to be a regular stream of visitors at Shambhu Maharaj's house. Many of them used to be professionals who had made a name for themselves. One of them, I remember was Menaka, a Bombay danseuse, who later married Lt. Gen. S.S. Sokhey. The main purpose of these visits, in the language of those days, was to get a little *polish* on one's attainments. Even his eldest brother, Achchan Maharaj (Birju's father) used to tell his disciples: I have given you what I have. For polish go to Shambhu. Women of the family, however proficient, never appeared on the stage in public.

One unforgettable event, I think of 1940, is the so-called All-India Music Conference – most such events were so publicized – held in the famous Baradari in Qaiserbagh (Lucknow), Achchan Maharaj was then in the Rampur Durbar and was billed to appear. Race horse owner Chandulal Shah, who was also connected with the film industry, had also come.

When Achchan Maharaj's name was announced there was a vociferous demand for his brother too. After some entreaties he came to the stage with hesitation and with folded hands and a bewitching smile urged the audience not to press him any more as it would not be in keeping with the dignity of his *bhaiyya* who was like father and guru to him. "However, to honour your wishes I would accompany him on the *tabla*", he said. Few had seen him in that role. At times it was difficult to say whether the applause was for the dancer or the accompanist. Many were also surprised that Achchan Baiyya, despite a bit heavy built, could be so agile on the stage and do so many *chakkars* with ease. Old Lucknawis recall Kalika Prasad accompanying his elder brother, Bindadin, on pakhawaj or tabla. Kalika would also keep a running commentary explaining the *bhavas* which were rather difficult to understand in those days.

Among the early disciples of Shambhu Maharaj after he shifted to Delhi were Maya Rao and Uma Sharma. Maya went to Moscow and came back after doing a course in choreography. Uma is a leading danseuse in Delhi and runs her own school.

Tabla reminds me of Ahmad Jan Thirakua and Kishen Maharaj of Banaras. Thirakuwa was the name given to him because of mesmeric movement of his fingers on the *tabla*. Soft and dignified in speech, he presented, at least to me, a quaint figure because of his butterfly moustache, churidar payjama, buttoned up long coat with two breast pockets with flaps and a Rampuri cap. After leaving the Rampur Durbar he taught at the Bhatkhande School.

Like Thirakuwa, Kishen Maharaj too is a wizard and is happily with us though with rare appearances perhaps because of age. Once the day he returned from a foreign trip he was to accompany Bare Ghulam Ali Khan at the Sapru House the same evening. As is usual bureaucrats with their wives occupy the front row at such functions. I happened to be in the second row. Khan Saheb was tuning the *tanpura* and *surmandal* when Kishen Maharaj came to the dais – usually the main performer is the last to take his seat

– greeted the audience and took his seat. As usual he was dressed in *Dhoti, chunnat kurta* and a big red bindi on his fair complexioned forehead. Suddenly a lady in the front row exclaimed. *"Hai itna khoobsoorat, main to margaee.*

Shuru kijiye, Khan Saheb, entreated someone. Gesturing towards a corner in the front row he said in the mike *zara inki guftagu khatma hojane dijiye.* The entire hall shouted silence, please.

I came to know Khan Saheb in Bombay in the early fifties. Congress Party used to be in my beat and reporters visited its office in Girgaum about midday. Vice-President K.K. Shah used to brief them. Most of the days I used to file the copy on the phone and then go to a flat opposite where Khan Saheb, when in Bombay, used to stay with a *gaanewali*. One day Shah appeared unnoticed, tapped me on the shoulder and wanted to know what I was intently looking at. When I told him all about it he said he would also like to meet Khan Saheb and after the briefing accompanied me. Most of the time Khan Saheb talked music. His callers, mostly eminent men and women in the profession, would exchange notes. Sometimes I used to accompany him to late evening sittings. His *Hari Om Tat Sat* became too popular.

Pandit Ravi Shankar and sitar have for long been synonymous. I came to know him when he was a producer in the All India Radio. I used to meet him there and sometimes walk with him to his house on the Ashok Road. Sometimes he used to depressingly talk about his work and the handicaps. To me it meant bureaucratic red tape. One day he said he was going to resign which he did soon. His first wife, Annapoorna, daughter of Alaudin Khan, was also proficient in sitar. I understand she now runs a school in Bombay and leads a reclusive life.

In the galaxy of dancers and musicians names of Ustad Fayyaz Khan, Bade Ghulam Ali Khan, Amir Khan, Kumar Gandharv, Heerabai Barodekar, Gangubai Hangal, Girija Devi, Siddheshwari Devi, Rasoolan Bai, Begam Akhtar, Pandit Ram Narayan, Chatur Lal and many others will always find an honoured position. To whichever school and discipline they belonged they reached that position by dint of hard work and dedication. Quite a few worked on intuition.

Of Fayyaz Khan, whose bust is installed at the entrance of the AIR building in Delhi, it is said he could fit in any company and sing anything besides classical, which was his forte Semi-classical, light classical and folk music came to him as easily as the classical. His *Bajuband khul khul jaye* was quite popular.

Pandit Omkar Nath Thakur also belongs to that genre. Endowed with robust health, a fine figure and a good voice he was a bit of a showman too. He was head of the department of music in the Banaras Hindu University for a time. Unlike other musicians of his time he used to have his own carpet and some other accessories spread on the stage. With an embroidered robe on his usual churidar and kurta and flowing hair he made an imposing figure.

It was the year in which the late Maharaja Banaras, Vibhuti Narayan Singh, got married in the early fifties. The Maharaja inaugurated the function in Lucknow and mentioned about his marriage in passing, with a Czechoslovakian girl friend. I sat through the programme till early morning.

Omkar Nath was the last artiste of the night. He began about three in the morning and ended with *Vaṅdemātaraṁ* at about 7 o'clock next morning. Singing of *Vaṅdemātaraṁ* and his famous *Jogi Mat Ja* still echo in my ears. Like other greats he had his own distinctive style. Amir Khan, who died in an accident in Kolkata, used to take a long time in warming up through *alaap* and delineation of the *rāga*.

If I mistake not it was Goswami Gopalji, a young, handsome man, who started the Swami Haridas Sammelan in Vrindavan. It used to be a rare gathering of professionals and the *rasiks* sat glued to their seats. Twice I attended and enjoyed these sammelans. On my repeated requests he once held the event in Delhi in V.P. House campus. It turned out to be a great draw for the connoisseurs. It was here that I last saw the doughty Sitara Devi dance her way to unstoppable acclaim. Her nephew (perhaps), Gopi Kishen, made a name as a dancer in glittering Mumbai.

Palghat Mani Iyer is a great name among drummers of the South. One of my journalist colleagues, who played *mridangam* and accompanied a Bharata Nāṭyam dancer, introduced me to him at a function where he was billed.

Names come rushing to mind when I think of those excelling in *thumri, dadra, chaiti, kajri* and *barahmasa*. Shobha Gurtu belonged to the younger generation. Mama Walwalkar used to be her accompanist on harmonium, which was banished from the AIR during I&B Minister B.V. Keskar's regime as it was not considered a suitable instrument. It returned after a long gap. Mahmoud

Dholpuri has already registered his name as a player of excellence on harmonium.

Rukmani Devi Arundale was a big name in Bharata Nāṭyam. She established Kalakshetra in Adyar near Chennai. I had the privilege of being her guest at Adyar when she was a member of the Rajya Sabha. Morarji Desai wanted to field her as a candidate for the President against Sanjiva Reddy.

Begum Akhtar, Ammi to many including me, made a name in *ghazal* singing. Like many others she was a woman of great grace and poise. Her diction, pronunciation and delineation of words, which matter, were superb. Not that she could not equally well sing other forms like *thumri, dadra and bandishes*. From Akhtari to Akhtari Bai to Begum Akhtar is a long story. In Delhi and Mumbai I attended quite a few of her private sittings in hotels and private houses. Dr. Brij Mohan Bajaj, who is connected with several social and cultural organizations, is one of her great admirers. She had left behind a number of talented disciples. Shanti Hiranand is perhaps the senior most. Dr. Bajaj instituted an award in Begum's memory. I happened to be on its top body which decided the awards. Unfortunately, it came to an end after a few years.

I don't know whether two institutions in Lucknow, *Bhairon ji ka Mela* and *Basant Panchmi* Congregation at *Shah Meena ka Mazar*, still continue. The former began in memory of Shambhu Maharaj's uncle, Bhairon Prasad, who died quite young. A temple dedicated to *Bhaironji* is just behind his ancestral house and a *mela* used to be held on the first Sunday of *Bhadon,* beginning of the rainy season. Many professionals attended it and made it a festival of dance and music.

So was the gathering at Shah Meena, adjacent to the Lucknow Medical College. Shambhu Maharaj used to be the presiding deity at both the places as he was guru and came from a noted gharana. Women from the nearby socalled red light district also attended the all-night congregation as the common belief was that if a professional does not get a chance to sing or dance even for a few minutes he or she will have a bad year.

It may be of some interest to know that *Maharaj* which became part of the name of male family members was a title bestowed on Thakur Prasadji, an uncle of Bindadinji, who was the *nrityaguru* of the then nawab of Oudh (Awadh). Bindadinji was seventy plus at the turn of the 19th century (1903-05) according to Abdul Halim

Sharar's *Ghuzishta Lakhanau*. He was a devotee of Lord Kṛishṇa and is said to have a vision of his. He was also a composer of *thumris* which invariably end with *Binda kahat*.

In forties and fifties even some non-Brahmin gurus added Maharaj to their names.

One can't forget Naina Devi while talking of *thumri*. She seemed to have imbibed its soul and its delicate sensual nature of singing. She came from a princely family and was fascinated by music from her younger days. She did what she could for the care of artistes in indigent circumstances.

A popular singer of light music in the 30s and 40s was Rahat Jan. He attained fame after he joined the team recruited by the British for the entertainment of troops in South East Asia.

I hope the purity of our heritage in classical music and dance, North Indian or South Indian – I don't know in which category Odisi fits in of which Samyukta Panigrahi and Kelu Charan Mohapatra were famous exponents – will be preserved and enriched. The way the Western influence is affecting the younger generation is not a good omen. Pollution is becoming visible.

16

Communication through Music

Shanti Hiranand

The dictionary meaning of the word 'communication' is the process of conveying information or knowledge from one individual to another or to a group. It would not be incorrect to say that music is one of the most significant means of communication known to human beings. It is said 'music hath charms to soothe the savage beast', so in fact, music communicates its message to animals as well.

Something of this is seen in the hymns of the *Ṛigveda*. Awestruck, delighted, terrified by the mighty forces of nature, our ancestors communicated with each other, and with the world for all time to come, their deep emotions on seeing the first glow of dawn, the radiance of the summer sun, the majesty of thunder, the mystery of the night, the cooling rays of the moon. Their outpourings were addressed to the elements-communicated to them, as it were. And the shared experience of reciting and hearing these hymns became for them a mode of creating a community – a word and concept not unrelated to the idea of communication, for surely communicating with someone is to establish a relationship, a sense of community. These early communications were oral renderings, and were poetic, philosophical and also musical. However the musical structures of the time were simple compared to those of today, using just 3-notes. Yet the power of those hymns is such that despite this very simple musical structure, the awesome grandeur of nature is communicated to us even today.

As people began to experiment more with sound, expanding their register beyond the initial Vedic 3-note structure, music as we know it today began to take shape. Rāga sangeet took many centuries to develop out of those initial Vedic hymns. But the urge to communicate – with their people, with the forces of nature, with the unseen 'shining ones', had now become a full-fledged pantheon of gods and it has remained that way. Barahmasa tradition obtained its shape in medieval time, and people in villages began singing kajris and chaitis to welcome and delight in the rains, and the summer's heat; in the temples, kirtankars sang praises of the Lord; in the rich courts and palaces, great musicians honed these village songs and transformed them into art to entertain and honour their patrons. They developed folk music into a fine art by adhering to the classical music tradition of rāga-rāginīs set in specific metrical setting. Tales are told of the legendary Tansen whose singing of Malhar communicated its message so effectively to the clouds that the rain would pour down in response to his music. Stories are also told of how hearing the sweet notes of music, the shy deer from the forests would come close and even permit a garland of flowers to be placed around their neck.

One of the most beautiful facets of communication in music is however the communicating of knowledge by guru to shishya. In music what is taught by the guru and what is learnt by the shishya is actually more than just the rāga structure, the bandish, or even the techniques of improvisation. These are no doubt very important, but they are only the tip of the iceberg. In fact what is communicated is far deeper. Through the taleem, a shishya learns to absorb and internalize a whole philosophy, a tradition, and a way of life. Thus it is not merely the voice that is shaped, not merely the knowledge of rāgas that is enriched, it is the self that is touched and made to flourish. In today's mechanical world where communication has become merely a functional thing, rather than the expression of the soul, this way of communicating, seena-ba-seena, heart to heart, so to speak, is unique and therefore all the more important.

The finest example of communication in and through, music is seen in the performances of great musicians. In the recent past we have the examples of great artistes like Ustad Bade Ghulam Ali Khan, Ustad Amir Khan, Pandit D.V. Paluskar, Ustad Fayyaz Khan and so many others. While listening to them, people experienced the richness of an emotional universe that was at the same time deeply spiritual. When the inimitable Queen of Ghazal, Begum Akhtar sang, each person in the audience felt she was addressing him personally, and felt deeply moved and uplifted.

Thus, through their performances, musicians communicate the experience of truth beauty and goodness (Satyaṁ, Śivaṁ, Sundaraṁ) to millions of people who listen to them. In this way, with communication through music, we might even say that the world becomes a better place.

17

Development and Growth of Dance as a Communication Discipline

Sucharita Khanna

A simple definition of development will be "an improvement in the quality of life obtained within the affirmation of cultural identity". Both as a performing artiste and a dance teacher I started looking into the aesthetic beauty of this art form in depth and found it linked inseparably with its rich literary foundation. Knowledge of discipline of dance and realization of its beauty and effect developed the artiste in me. My mind was tuned to grasp a very wide and holistic perspective of knowledge – cosmology to science of metallurgy, while looking at the bronze image of Naṭarāja. The ultimate of Hindu mythology lies in the theory of aesthetics where *Satyaṁ, Śivaṁ* and *Sundaraṁ* work in harmony with each other as trinity. The concept of the truth, auspiciousness and beauty give a strong base and edifice to the structure of dance.

In early times, there were no classroom studies and teaching. The world in itself was the stage, open sky provided the roof and shelter to the artistes. The divine sound of *Om* created the power by giving life and movement to all who exist. That was the rhythm of the universe, where lies the actual essence of human being. Temple and its compound became the first classrooms for the students of dance. Chanting of mantras provided the holy music through which one could build communication silently with his/her inner self making him/her realize his/her true divine nature. Deep meditation helped the process further. Mythological symbols, sculptures, iconography and paintings became major tools of communication by which understanding of literature and practical art became possible. Temples also served as community centres, institutions, places of worship, theatres for entertainment and became major centres for bringing people together.

The stage on which dance was performed was considered to be a temple – place of worship – because all classical dances which exist in India have been temple dances. Now they are not confined to the four walls of temple but have a regular ritualistic feature still present in their soul.

The objective of dances was to create a bridge or establish communion between the human and the divine. Accordingly Indian philosophy, traditions, legends and mythology are constantly being revived and lived through dance. Even those who are not educated or have no access to literature are able to perceive the story or an event which the dancer is performing. Action in visual form is always better received than theoretical discourse.

Let us recall the masterpieces of such *rūpas,* which have to this day continued to inspire artistic minds from the period of Mohenjo-daro culture till today. They are divine in themselves, a constant source of energy, an inspiration through which journey of dance could proceed on its ultimate path. These are mainly, the cosmic dancer Śiva as Naṭarāja, *Ardhanārīśvara* – the integrated personality of the male and female principle or the Divine Couple; Harihara as Vishṇu and Śiva combined; Rādhā and Kṛishṇa – the divine loving couple in human form; and Durgā, the supreme power of energy; four-faced Brahmā – God of four cardinal directions and Daśāvatāra – ten incarnations of Vishṇu.

ŚIVA

In Śaiva tradition, images of Naṭarāja represent the most exalted aspect of Śiva – a metaphor for the cosmic cycle of creation and destruction and the individual cycle of birth and re-birth. The dance of Śiva is identified with the *Pañchākshara,* the five syllables (*na-ma-śi-vā-ya* = Namaḥ Śivāya). In his feet *na,* in his navel *ma,* in his shoulder *śi,* in his face is *vā,* and in his head is *ya.* According to *Unmai Vilakkam* (verse 36), creation arises from drum, protection proceeds from the hand of hope, from fire proceeds destruction, the foot held aloft gives mukti, is the same as *anugraha*- release, the fourth hand points to the lifted foot, the refuge of the soul.

Śiva's cosmic dance represents his five activities – *pañchakriyā* viz. *sṛishṭi* (creation), *stithi* (preservation), *samhāra* (destruction), *tirobhava* (wailing) and *anugraha* (release). These separately considered, are the activities of deities – Brahmā, Vishṇu, Rudra, Maheśvara and Sadāśiva. The dance represents his rhythmic activity as the source of all movements within the cosmos which is represented by the glory of halo around his famous Naṭarāja figure.

Another aspect of his dance is well defined as *Ardhanārīśvara*, the power of *Purusha* and *Śakti* combine. The *lāsya* mode is beautifully added to the violent *tāṇḍava* of Śiva which reminds us about this popular theme in *kāvya* literature. There is a graphic description of Śiva as dancing in *Ardhanārīśvara* form, dividing *tāṇḍava* and *lāsya* in his two halves of the body, by his delicate *aṅgahāras* on one side and terribly violent movements on the other side. In this aspect, Śiva took Pārvatī as part of himself to show the unity between nature and God, which together indicates the dynamic power of *Purusha* and *Śakti*.

VISHṆU

The concept of Vishṇu being the preserver of the universe came relatively late in Hinduism. Presumably, it sprang from two other beliefs: that men attain salvation by faithfully following predetermined paths of duty, and the powers of good and evil (gods and demons) who are in contention for domination over the world.

Vishṇu is believed to have been eternal and omni-present as an all – pervading spirit which had been in existence, associated with primaeval waters, even before the creation of the Universe. He is the protector of all living creatures in the world.

The fundamental principle of education is well explained by the example of the *Daśāvatāra*- in relation to the development of society and its growth. Each *avatāra* plays an important role and has its own significance. This concept is corner stone of Hindu philosophy and each *avatāra* happens to be an incarnation of God for material well-being and moral upliftment of mankind.

The notable aspects of incarnations are that God comes from an unmanifest state to a manifest state, that is, *amūrta to mūrta rūpa*. The incarnations may vary in number from text to text but it is obvious that every incarnation happens to be a decent of God on earth[1] and not of ascent of man unto God and the ultimate purpose of incarnation is the establishment of *dharma* and to punish the wicked.[2]

Also, when Vishṇu transformed himself into *Mohinīrūpa,* Śiva got enamoured with her beauty, not knowing the actual reality. Śiva and Vishṇu thus became one and formed the divine aspect of manifestation as Harihara.

RĀDHĀ-KṚISHṆA

Lord Kṛishṇa is the eighth incarnation of Lord Vishṇu. He is the supreme statesman, warrior, hero, teacher and philosopher and author of the *Bhagavadgītā*. He has been called 'the divine ecstatic' because of the sound of his flute which is absorbed in the calls of the divine. Kṛishṇa's youthful dalliances with the *gopis* are interpreted as symbolic of love interplay between the God and the human soul.

Simultaneously, when we talk of love, the name of the only divine couple Rādhā and Kṛishṇa comes into our mind. Rādhā's intense love for Kṛishṇa and their relationship are often interpreted as the mortal's quest for union with the divine. This kind of love is of the highest form of devotion in Vaishnavism, and is symbolically represented as the bond between beloved and her lover. In other words, we can say, their divine love reminds us of the harmonious and loving union of the divine female and male. They become one and are depicted as Rādhā Mādhava, that is, in one form, where aesthetically speaking the two persons of opposite sex get so inseparably united that their duality is lost. Since medieval period this evergreen love theme has engrossed poets, painters, musicians, dancers and all Kṛishṇa devotees alike.

Each divine form or *avatāra* plays an important role and has its own significance. The devotion and dedication towards the divine with a rich backdrop of literature inspired the artist to create these beautiful undying images each with a narrative story and mythological setting. The dancing figures of divinities are based on mythological narratives or on the *dhyānarūpas*. In order to evaluate the iconographic aspects of these figures one has to be acquainted with mythology as well as the *dhyānas* referred to in the iconographical texts. The mythological narratives are mostly found in the *Purāṇas* and in *Āgama* literature and as such, most of the narrative panels showing dancing divinities should be assigned to a date later than the compilation or creation of *Purāṇas* and *Āgamas*. On the basis of these stories, we find a situation, which compelled a god to dance. These *kathas* underlie the projection of images and give us a clear idea of different themes which are the subject matter of dance by the chief gods. The gods are seen dancing benignly when they are pleased. When they are happy they dance in ecstasy. But at times when they are furious, they present themselves in terrific mood. Thus, the theme of a dance and its predominating rasa (delight) governs the creation of figures or forms.

On the basis of these examples, we often think in terms of God creating us but it should dawn on us that it is we who visualize and create different forms of Gods and Goddesses. We realise our purest qualities but are unable to accept them as 'self'. We initially view them outside us and call these our Gods. At a deeper level it is a vision of self. Our highest idea of self which we are unable to claim within us, we project as gods. Our perspective is essentially the human perspective and we project gods with all divine qualities that we too are capable of if only we recognize the potential within. However, we give these qualities a human name and form. We understand, for example, life force and its supremacy and awareness through different forms of Śiva; we understand power and its strength through Kālī and Durgā. Our purest visions of self become our gods.

Bharata Nāṭyam practised in the temples and in the various community centres was associated with a strong ethnic and religious allegiance. Such a religious allegiance had no scope for providing Bharata Nāṭyam with a professional status in the main stream. This art is a means of spiritual elevation both for the dance and the audience. It is also an attempt to embody the divine beauty, charm, rhythms and symbols that presumably exist in heaven.

The journey of dance is continuing and proves this art form to be a purely communicating way of the deepest and most lasting level. The dance is the mother of arts. It removes the limitations of the body, extinguishes the consciousness and pours the divine spirit into the dancer. This provides the artiste all the scope to create a manifestation of his/her own soul.

In recent times there has been a tremendous development and improvement in the field of dance. The society, dancers and institutions promoting dance, are slowly weeding out the unwanted aspect of the *devadasi* tradition and the stigma attached with this dance form.

Actually speaking no one knows about the origin of unchanging pattern called tradition. There has always been change inherent in the flow of all creative arts and what we create today as an innovation, might solidify into tradition in time. If one is to reenact the same old times, without an iota of change, how can it be called a living art? Idea of development and change is inherent in creative arts. The only consideration to keep in mind is to stick to established aesthetic values and maintain their purest forms. The underlying principle in every art happens to be beauty, and its aesthetic quotient. Anything beautifully presented has aesthetic value and it is to be enjoyed.[3] One should not bring parochial considerations in evaluation of art.

Dance depicts this very unceasing rhythm of the universe that lives at once in space and time. Artiste and his/her work of art happen to be one and the same thing. In dance, rhythmic patterns of movements, the plastic sense of space and a vivid representation of the world seen and imagined are all created by the artiste with his/her own body, giving expression to his inner experience. Firstly, the vision is confined merely to perceptions, emotions and thoughts but when we transcend the limitation of our body, mind and intellect then one realizes one's inner self. This gives us a valuable message that 'nothing generates in vacuum, but grows in the womb of tradition'. It does not replace it; it transforms it.

The present is modernized tradition, a new wave in the ocean of time. If the modern rejects the whole of tradition it ceases to be modern; it becomes rootless and anaemic, glossy but ephemeral. If tradition does not eschew the obsolete by modernizing itself, it ceases to be tradition, it becomes sterile, a stagnant pool of decay and degeneration.

In my opinion there have already been vast innovative changes and improvements in the Bharata Nāṭyam scene today, compared to the fifties and sixties. This dance form has been choreographed in contemporary style yet keeping its classical tradition intact. This aspect is rarely seen in other Indian classical dance forms. When you compare Bharata Nāṭyam with other dance forms and their progress or development, one should bear in mind that

Bharata Nāṭyam style has been a source of inspiration for others to develop their own styles.

Bharata Nāṭyam has already gone through various evolutionary changes and since it has a long standing antiquity compared to other styles, it certainly has come to a state where it can smoothly fly to a high level without much deviation. Other styles are still at a take off stage. They have drawn a lot from Bharata Nāṭyam repertoire pattern and have learnt how a solo could be arranged in such a way the it could take the whole programme to a crescendo.

Today, dance is an important tool of communication with oneself and with others. Understanding of its development and growth would enhance our ability to express ourselves in a perfect manner in any field or discipline.

NOTES AND REFERENCES

1. The *Vishṇu Purāṇa* asserts that the people born on the Indian soil are entitled to the status higher than that of the Gods (suratvāt) (R.V.).
2. *Bhagavadgītā*, IV.7.
3. 'A thing of beauty is joy for ever.' Kālidāsa makes Śiva tell Pārvatī, in his *Kumārasambhava,V.36* that "beauty does not lead one to the path of sin", is not a deviational statement (R.V.).

18

Bharata Nāṭyam – Speaking in the Present Tense

Malavika Sarukkai

What is the solo Bharata Nāṭyam tradition that we have inherited over the centuries?

It was at its best perhaps when presented by a legendary dancer like Tanjavur Balasaraswati who imbued it with the passion of sensuality and spirituality. Performing the *mārgaṁ* (repertoire) was for her, as she said, a journey from the outer pavilions, mandapas, of the temple into the innermost sanctum, the *garbha-griha*. And into her inner journey she drew the *rasikas*.

Today, however, I think when the Bharata Nāṭyam performance is not invested with the deeper resonances underlying the classical, it easily becomes mere entertainment – dance that pleases without touching deeper chords in the viewers.

Many equate Bharata Nāṭyam with just its repertoire – a repertoire that evolved under certain social and historical circumstances. They do not recognize the dance form's inherent resilience for change. This narrow vision seems to me to disinherit Bharata Nāṭyam of its vast potential. To quote Dr. Kapila Vatsyayan "Indian traditions have an inbuilt mechanism of change...." This is crucial. For the Indian artiste, tradition and change are part of the same flow, two innate rhythms that explore discipline and freedom. Only when seen together can the river of tradition run deep, reinventing itself. As a performing artist my concern is with *tradition and change* not tradition or change.

This river of Bharata Nāṭyam has seen much change through the centuries – from temple to court to proscenium stage. The viewing context changed when Bharata Nāṭyam shifted out of the court and onto the proscenium stage. This shift has empowered the female artiste to construct her own aesthetics instead of 'offering' the dance for pleasuring the male gaze. This underlines the significance today to collectively repossess our tradition both as practitioners of the art form and as viewers.

I have been a *sadhika* of this dance form for decades, forever searching, forever grateful. Through a process of internalization, I attempt to re-present the style and to recover the female form – investing it with passion, sensuality, aesthetics and beauty of spirit – but always within the parameters of the classical. I wish to bring to the language of dance a vital energy *that speaks in the present tense*; this I owe as a practitioner of a great tradition that *can rejuvenate itself by adapting to flux. Else, it will lose its vitality.* I believe my style of solo Bharata Nāṭyam is rooted in the sacred works with the classical alphabet and allows for interpretations with contemporary energies. This empowers it with immediacy. For me, Bharata Nāṭyam is a language that **speaks in the present tense.**

Bharata Nāṭyam is a powerful and evocative language of dance when articulated through an energized and sensitive body and mind. And then it reveals its vast potential. The canvas stretches to hold new visions and innovations.

Over the last twenty-five years I have been greatly rewarded by the overwhelming response from my audiences both in India and abroad. Many streams of aesthetics, poetry, philosophy and emotional impulse flow together to create dance. Art experience is about encountering metaphors and making creative leaps. And critics and others who merely look for a literal 'understanding' of the piece, I think, lose out on the richness of the experience of *rasa*.

It is only after years of living with a style and internalizing it that I feel one can create from within. In 1986 I started doing my own choreography. I was finding my own voice, my own rhythm. Feeling is seminal to my choreography. And this is what my dance communicates. Dancer and audience meet in spaces of shared emotions.

Nowadays Bharata Nāṭyam is being constantly questioned about its relevance and validity in todays changing times. I believe Bharata Nāṭyam is a living, breathing art form. As I have said, for the Indian artiste, tradition and change are part of the same flow. And Bharata Nāṭyam is the language of my training with which I express my innermost feelings.

Being a woman artiste and working in India, a country which has always encouraged a plurality of approach, a 'complex seeing', I feel the need to grant the 'woman' in dance multidimensions. The evolution of her persona changed with the changing tides of social and historical events. In the traditional repertoire she was depicted as a *nayika*, a woman mostly seen in a love relationship with a man. Over the years this too became cloaked in spiritual longing, at times contrived and grossly misplaced. Of course the Varnam, when performed in the best sense of the word, granted her another dimension of *sringara bhakti*, i.e. love for the Supreme Lord. Broadly speaking, the emotions uncovered in a performance by the dancer and for the viewer were the spiritually infused emotions as expressed in the Varnam, and the many nuances of a man- woman relationship as expressed in the *padams* and *javalis*.

Doing my own choreography impelled me to get closer in touch with myself. There was a growing awareness of other areas which needed validation. Besides, the role of patron – dancer had changed as also the central position of a man in a woman's world. The canvas of Bharata Nāṭyam which till now seemed richly filled with the emotions of *sringara* started to expand revealing other spaces. As a woman and as an artiste, I was questioning myself, trying to redefine the areas of my search. Other emotional spaces needed attention, and through dance I gave expression to them . I explored tentatively the transience of life in Kashi, the deep calling of a woman's primary instinct to nurture in Thimmaka, and a mothers fortitude when confronted with the call of destiny in Aprachanam.

Over the past 15 years there has been a shift in my interpretations and in the thematic content of my productions in the Bharata Nāṭyam idiom. In the need to connect with myself and to give expression to concerns within me, I find my repertoire in both *nritta* and *abhinaya* has undergone a change.

Doing new work within the expanding canvas of Bharata Nāṭyam demands great intelligence and imagination. No structure is given and one cannot resort to familiar patterns. It is then of utmost importance to keep in mind 'auchityaṁ' appropriateness and the need to evoke 'rasa', contemplative savouring. I believe these two principles root the artiste and give stability to the production enabling her to repossess her tradition in the light of contemporary awareness.

Living in today's times I feel a need to respond to the world around us, as a human being and as an artiste. To engage ones creative energies in sensitizing oneself and the audience to deeper resonances and larger perspectives. I do not see the classical art form of Bharata Nāṭyam as an entertainment, something the audience watches passively. But, rather as a language of dance that takes the audience to other levels. Allowing the audience to temporarily let go of themselves. Art experience frees one from the binds of everyday life. Especially if one looks around at the social environment we are living in, the stressed lifestyles, the pressures of work and of having to balance career and personal life. Then, I think, it is even more imperative to allow inputs into our lives from the world of the arts.

Indian dance works with time and space. *Nritta*, pure dance, is for me movement connecting points of stillness – *sthiti gati*. From the still centre dance movements radiate outward and return to the centre. Using the body the dancer stretches movement over time. There are two kinds of energy a dancer can generate within the body – the *rājasika*, which is the more explosive and physically seen energy by the audience and the *sāttvika*, the more controlled, contemplative energy which is more felt than seen by the audience. When the *sāttvika* dance energy flows uninterrupted through the mind and body of the dancer it is as if she is lit from within. Lit with another luminosity.

In painting or sculpture the artist works with an external medium whereas for the dancer her body is her medium. With her body she sculpts space with dance design. Filling and painting space, investing it with the sacred.

In my choreography I lay emphasis on the path of movement as it etches space. Space is thereby energized, and lives. And meaning is communicated. Depending on the context and delivery technique, movements in themselves – independent of facial expressions — can create resonances of emotion.

Abhinaya, expressional dance, is the second aspect of Bharata Nāṭyam. To make a tradition speak in the present tense, in the moment, the dancer has to recreate in the present. Giving to dance a live force. To infuse an item with *prana* or breath is to feel the flow of sap permeating the body. The membrane of the body is filled with *sāttvika* energy. When dance is deep felt, performed with passion and one's whole being is invested with such energy – tradition lives.

For the Indian classical dancer the need to evoke 'rasa' a heightened awareness is of primary importance. This underlying concept influences all levels of performance and presentation. It is this unique quality that transforms the physical body even as it celebrates it. Transforms it from mere **performance to experience**. And it is through this passionate and deep felt dancing experience that the classical dancer communicates to audiences all over the world.

19

Kuchipuḍī Dance as Means of Communication

Raja Radha Reddy

Dance is a powerful instrument of communication and means of cultural integration in a nation. Its unique capacity to combine ancient ideologies and traditions with modern aspirations and trends helps peoples' and nations' transition smoothly, simultaneously equipping them for aesthetic, social, spiritual and other functions.

Dance of a country plays a significant role in the consolidation and development of its culture. It is an essential part of a country's heritage – its civilization and culture. It forms a binding force of communication by which present generation learns from its past. A nation without dance tradition has truly nothing to fall back upon, nothing to draw inspiration from. Dance conveys history of the greatest souls of the past to the present generation.

India is one of the very few nations in the world whose present is not de-linked from its past or its roots. It is one of the most ancient civilizations of the world rooted in its glorious tradition of dances. This elevates dance to the status of a national symbol. Classical dance styles here provide a distinguishing experience of India that was, is and will be.

In India Vedas are the oldest source of knowledge of dance and other arts of ancient people. They are believed to be the Divine Knowledge received by the *ṛishis* from the supreme Being.

According to Hindu mythology, at the beginning of Tretayuga, people were leading a life of misery and were going wayward on account of being driven by evil desires and were degenerating by subjecting themselves to the elemental passions of lust, greed, rancour, etc. Seeing this, Lord Indra along with the other devas (gods), approached Brahmā (the creator of the Universe and four Vedas) and requested him to create a source of entertainment which could be heard, seen and enjoyed by all sections of people and which would help them lead a divinely ordained life.

Hence a Fifth Veda called *Nāṭya Veda* was promulgated which exemplified righteousness, brought prosperity, caused fame, contained instructions and comprehended all activities forming a guide to the future generations as well.[1]

This *Nāṭya Veda* was taught to Bharata Muni along with his hundred sons (disciples), who promulgated dance to different parts of the country. Each part of the country due to its religious and cultural influences developed its own style of dance. Though these dance styles are very different from each other, there is a striking similarity between all of them. These classical dance styles came to be known as Kathak in northern India, Odīssī in Orissa, Bharata Nāṭyam in Tamil Nadu, Mohinīaṭṭam and Kathakali in Kerala and Kuchipuḍī in Andhra Pradesh. What eventually emerged in South India was a culture that drew on elements from the north and yet had its own distinct flavour. A magnified symbol of this synthesis is the image of Naṭarāja (The Lord of Dance). Lord Naṭarāja has been described thus:

> For Naṭarāja (Śiva) the whole universe is the body (or the movement of his body is the universe itself), which is Āngika Abhinayaṁ, all languages are his speech (Vāchika Abhinayaṁ); heavenly bodies like the moon and stars are his jewels (this is Āhārya Abhinayaṁ); I bow to Lord Śiva who is the embodiment of pacific expression of emotions (Sāttvika-Abhinayaṁ).[2]

Lord Śiva has been compared with a dancer/actor whose four abhinayas (medium of communication) are Āṅgikaṁ (bodily gestures), Vāchikaṁ (words and songs), Āhāryaṁ (costume) and Sāttvikaṁ (pacific expression). Hence came the following expression:

> Thus is our Lord the Dancer King; Thus is our Dance
> This is our hoary heritage; This is our holy heritage

To bestow the human beings with Purushārthas, i.e. Dharma, Artha, Kāma, Moksha (The divine path of life), the *Nāṭya Veda* was created out of the auxiliaries of the other four Vedas. Recitation was taken from the *Ṛigveda*, Music from *Sāmaveda*, Gestural representation from *Yajurveda* and aesthetic emotions from *Atharvaveda*.[3]

The *Ṛigveda*, the earliest of the four Vedas, describes rituals where, in order to establish correspondence between the human body and its several parts and the macrocosm, a number of gestures were used. There are references such as: "With my hands and arms outstretched, I invoke this sky, with the palm facing down and fingers pointing to the earth, I invoke the goddess earth." These were elementary but powerful expressions.

By the time of the *Yajurveda*, the chief text of rites and rituals, a whole language in gestures had developed. Among the objects that could be suggested were plants, animals, birds, earth, fire, water, sky, human beings, and their emotions, the sun, moon, etc. Thus through this language of gestures a whole world of mythology could be recreated in kinetic visual terms.

By the 2nd century AD this gestural terminology was made into a language with a definite grammar, vocabulary and syntax. Also at this stage was composed *Nāṭyaśāstra*, the first text of Indian dance, drama, music, literature and aesthetics. Bharata, the author of the *Nāṭyaśāstra*, lists both single and double hand gestures. He then indicates the several ways in which each of them can be used to describe situations, suggest objects, indicate emotions or be symbolic of higher states of consciousness. Alongside is another group of hand gestures which are used not for purposes of meaning but only for embellishment and rendering movement as design. The first category of hastas or mudrās, as they are sometimes erroneously called, are Abhinaya Hastas, i.e. those which are related to histrionics or acting. The second group is called Nṛitta Hastas, i.e. those which are used in pure dance but have no meaning.

An Abhinaya Hasta can indicate several types of meaning, depending upon the direction of the palm and fingers in relation to the body level at which these hands are used. For instance 'Patākā Hasta', the outstretched palm with the thumb touching the index finger means a banner. A banner can be indicative of many things. The hand once used in this fashion can suggest a king; it can suggest you when the palm is at a chest level and pointing at a spectator; the palm when facing outward with the fingers pointing downwards towards the earth can mean ground. There are various permutations of the Patākā like the Tripatākā and Ardha Patākā that evoke a host of other things.

The Ardha Chandra or half moon develops from Patākā, the only difference being that instead of the thumb touching the index finger, it is stretched out. This gesture can suggest the half moon itself, falling water, and the wind or sundry aspects of nature. Similarly Kartarī Mukha (mouth of the scissor) is like the Ardha Patākā but the index finger and the middle finger are separated out like the ends of a scissor. This can show the traversing of a path.

The hand gestures are a whole universe unto themselves. This perfection in gestural communication has been achieved to a degree of excellence in Indian dance and can also be witnessed in dance styles of South East Asia particularly Thailand, Indonesia and Cambodia.

The great poet Kālidāsa has also written:

> Dance (nāṭyam) often provides a unified forum for universal entertainment for discerning people of different tastes.[4]

Kuchipuḍī Dance of Andhra Pradesh originated in the Kuchipuḍī village in the Kṛishṇa district of Andhra Pradesh. The village had been granted by the kings to a group of brāhmaṇa families. The male members of these families became famous artistes in dance and drama. With austerity and conviction, Kuchipuḍī artistes spread the art of Kuchipuḍī dance in their unique style in several parts of the world.

Kuchipuḍī Dance is subtle in its bestowal, sprightly in its technique, unique in its manners and universal in its appeal. It is a poetic expression of life's variegated moods. It speaks through manifold rhythmic patterns, melodic gestures and subtle facial expressions, creating a new world of ecstasy and gives an ethereal experience. Kuchipuḍī Dance consists of a combination of speech, music, and imitative gestures (mudrās). It is an art which uses bodily motion to convey thoughts: as in speech the tongue articulated words, so while dancing the body sways and gesticulates into meaning.

Due to their expertise in dance and music, speech, imitative gestures and literature, the Kuchipuḍī dancers have become experts in communication. The dancers through their abhinayam (act of communication) convey the meaning of a play or a song or a verse. Any reaction to one's own pains and pleasure in daily life is not abhinaya, but when the same is undertaken to be portrayed on stage, where the dancers suppress their own identity as if they are real characters it is known as abhinaya. This in turn is seen, heard, felt and experienced by the spectator. The dancer creates a feeling in the minds of the spectators, where what they see on stage is the original character in flesh and blood. Once this happens the eyes of the dancer become the mirror of his/her soul. So powerful is dance as means of communication, that when a skilled dancer communicates effectively, the audience experiences Ānanda (bliss).

In olden days when no transportation facilities were available, Kuchipuḍī dancers (Bhāgavathars = Bhāgavatas) used to travel from place to place, loading on bullocks, their baggage with idols, groceries, etc. on one side and costumes, stage properties, etc. on the other side, performing at various places, selecting the subject to suit to local customs.

There is a famous tale of the Kuchipuḍī dancers in the Machupallī kaifiyat, a court document of AD 1505. According to it, the Kuchipuḍī artists on their way to Vijayanagaram, stayed at Siddhavatam, which was ruled by Sambata Guruvaraju, the local ruler and an agent of Vīranarasiṁharāyā, the King of Vijayanagara Kingdom. Pained by the atrocities of Sambata Guruvaraju, the Kuchipuḍī dancers enacted his misdeeds before the King. The communication by the Kuchipuḍī dancers was so strong that the King ordered the beheading of Sambata Guruvaraju.

Abhinaya, the act of communication is four fold. When done by means of various limbs, it is known as *Āṅgika Abhinaya;* it is *Vāchika Abhinaya,* when done by means of voice and speech; it is *Sāttvika Abhinaya* when done by means of emotional reactions; and *Āhārya Abhinaya* when done by means of make-up and costumes. There is a famous sloka in the *Nāṭyaśāstra*:

> The dancers sing the song and express the meaning thereof with their hands. They express the feelings therein with the eyes and simulataneously give the 'tāla' (rhythm) with their feet.[5] Wherever the hand moves the glance should follow it; where the glance is pointing, the mind should follow it; where the mind is fixed, there the bhāva (emotion) arises; when the bhāva is expressed, then there is rasa (sentiment).[6]

There is no wisdom or knowledge, art or craft, device or action that cannot be communicated through dance. Dance is the ultimate tool of communication. It is not limited by language, caste or creed. While preaching universal brotherhood, justice and truth, it also succeeds in helping people experience spirituality. It finds its source in movements and gestures which were mediums of communication in the primaeval times. Dance is fit to be the starting point of all literary progress.

Dance is not merely a form of entertainment; it has become a treasure of communication for the people to take a divine path, to lead a divine life. It leads them to sound health, a life without any disease or pain. It gifts them mental peace (peace of mind without disturbance) and Ānanda (bliss) within self. Today in 21st century it would be a good idea to look back and see the strides taken in the last century and from that vintage point foresee the steps to be taken in the future while learning from the past. It is evident that dance is a form of communication that encompasses words and yet contains all that cannot be expressed by words. It is a journey that originates in reality, roller coasters through imagination and ends in spirituality.

NOTES AND REFERENCES

1. *Nāṭyaśāstra,* vol. 2, chap. 1, 8-16,
त्रेतायुगे सम्प्रवृत्ते मनोवैर्वस्वतस्य तु
ग्राम्य धर्मप्रवृत्ते तु कामलोभवशंगते।
....
नाट्यवेदं ततश्चक्रे, चतुर्वेदसम्भवम्। 16
see also, Kavita Nagpal, f.n. 1.
2. आंगिकं भुवनं यस्य, वाचिकं सर्व वाड्मयम्(आहार्यं चन्द्रतारादि तं वंदे सात्त्विकं शिवम्।
3. ऋग्यजुस्सामवेदेभ्यो वेदच्चाथर्वणः क्रमात् (पाठ्याभिनयं गीतं रसान् संगृह्य पद्मजारचयच्छास्त्रमिदं धर्मकामार्थमोक्षदम्।
see also, Kavita Nagpal, f.n. 2.
4. Kālidāsa, *Mālavikāgnimitra*, act I .4; नाट्यं भिन्नरुचेर्जनस्य बहुधाप्येकं समाराधनम्
5. कण्ठेनालम्भयेत् गीतं हस्तेनार्थ प्रदर्शयेत्;
चक्षुर्भ्यां दर्शयेत् भावं पादाभ्यां तालमाचरेद्
6. *cited in Nāṭyaśāstra*, vol. 1 p. 21 as
तदुक्तमादिभरते-
यतो हस्तस्ततो दृष्टिः यतो दृष्टिस्ततो मनः
यतो मनस्ततो भावो यतो भावस्ततो रसः।

BIBLIOGRAPHY

Apparao, P.S.R., *Abhinaya Darpanam.*
Bharata's *Nāṭyaśāstra.*
Vatsyayan, Kapila, *Mudrās the Language of Hands.*

20

Kathak Dance – An Effective Medium of Communication

Shovana Narayan

Gestures are inextricably linked with dance as a means of communication. Gestures are a language that knows no boundaries and dance too is a language beyond boundaries. However, gestures cannot be divorced from emotions for the two together create and communicate an idea or a feeling or thought. Universality of emotions and gestures cannot be disputed, equally undisputable is the fact that some gestures may convey different meanings in different cultural contexts. But emotions and emotional responses cannot change even in the context of cultures. This feature is the only continuing reality binding ages, cultures and continents. A smile is a smile conveying friendship and sympathy and, on the other hand, anger is anger whose meaning is unmistakably loud and clear. Do we need to have a language of words to convey the meaning of anger?

Indian classical solo dances use a large vocabulary of gestures and combine them with emotional responses convey various meanings. Originating from ritualistic dance as overwhelming emotional and physical response to the great devotional upsurge within, in course of time the grammar of skilled solo dances evolved and each situation and each character described/describes while enacting sequences from the lives of deities. Over a period of time this developed into a well-defined and codified language of gestures, including hand gestures, that became inextricably associated with Indian dances.

All classical dances in India are therefore medium of communication of ideas through the language of gestures and emotions. This has always been one of the most effective visual manifestations of the inner upsurge of emotions. So intense must have been the developments in the area of performing arts that it motivated an extensive codification of limbs, hand gestures and emotions enunciated in the over two thousand years old Indian treatise on theatrics, the *Nāṭyaśāstra*. In its scope, treatment, codification of all limbs of performing arts, this treatise on dramaturgy remains unparalleled till date. It is but another matter of interest that regionalization of classical dances began only about a thousand years ago.

In fact, it is a truism that the frontiers of dance cannot ever be static for dance is a dynamic process. The history of classical dance has seen several changes, first in its journey towards classicality and then in its content and form. In this voyage into the past, the well known opening story of the *Nāṭyaśāstra* gives an indication to the dance scene that existed two thousand years ago. This story seems to indicate that dance was only a small part of an overall musical production. But within this, recognition had been given to individualism, skill and dexterity of the performer. At the same time it is also necessary to take note of the outstanding dance skills of Āmrapālī, Śalvatī, Padmāvatī, Rūpā Ghoshā, to name a few. While the first three dancers were contemporaries of Lord Buddha in 6th century BC (centuries before the *Nāṭyaśāstra* was written), the last mentioned belongs to the Gupta period of Indian history (namely 4th-5th centuries AD). Thus it can reasonable be argued that individual dance style did exist even prior to the *Nāṭyaśāstra*.

The period of the *Nāṭyaśāstra* is also taken to be the period when the *Mahābhārata* epic was consolidated in a written form. Interestingly, the Ādiparva and the Anuśāsnikaparva of the *Mahābhārata* do mention the 'kathakas'. But it is usually argued that the term 'kathaka' is a generic one for any storyteller or bard. To support this line of approach verses from the *Mahābhārata* with reference to 'kathakas', are quoted. However it may also be of interest to study the line of argument put forth by Arthur Berrierdale Keith who stated that the 'kathakas' communicated in two distinct categories: one who communicated through verbal medium alone and were therefore broadly known as 'pāṭhakas' and the second who communicated through the language of gestures and should be recognized as the performer 'kathakas'. In this context an examination of the recently discovered Prakrit text of 4th century BC becomes significant. In this text what is of interest are the terms 'savvo kathiko bhiṅgāra natenam' for here the term 'savvo' stands for all, 'kathiko' for the kathakas, 'bhiṅgāra' for śṛingāra and 'natenam' for dance. These put together clearly indicate that the 'kathakas' referred here were a group of dancers known for their graceful performances.

> *maggasira-suddhapakkhe nakkhate Vārānasīye nayariye uttarpurathime disibhāge Gangāye mahānadīye taṭe savvo-kathiko bhiṅgāra-natenam tise stuti kayam yehi rāyā Adināho bhavenam passayi*
>
> (Ancient Prakrit Text, 4th century BC)

> (i.e. In the month of Māgha, in the period of Śukla Paksha Nakshatra, to the north of Varanasi, on the banks of the Ganges, the śṛingāra dance of the 'kathakas' pleased Lord Ādinātha).

Keith's line of reasoning is further borne out by the less quoted verse from Maurya period namely *'nṛityadharmmaṁ kathakaścha devalokaṁ....'*, which is even more of a clear indication of dance being the 'dharma' (duty) of 'kathakas'.

The living dance scene in various regions of the sub-continent evident from a discussion of the four 'vṛittis' in the *Nāṭyaśāstra*, sowed the seeds of the classical dance scene that flowered subsequently. Regional variations with individual identity became a recognizable reality only a millennium later. But was it then or a little later, can be open to debate.

In addition to being the vehicle of self-expression, most of our classical dances also have been utilized to convey a value system desirable for mankind. In addition, a dance form such as Kathak also mirrors key elements of Indian philosophy in its basic stance as well as pirouettes. If Bharata Nāṭyam and Kuchipuḍī seem to depict triangles in their basic stances, 'kathakas' basic stance is an upward moving arrow desirous of union with the Almighty. The basic arm position with the 'Dhyāna Mudrā Hasta' at chest level so very identifiable with Kathak, which mirrors the 'Dhyāna Mudrā' of yoga. The pirouettes, once again so characteristic of Kathak, are but visual representation of the basic Indian philosophy of the cycle of life and death, the 'Jīvana Chakra' and the 'Kāla Chakra'. The 's' movement and the serpentine gait of Oḍissī and Maṇipuri are reflections of the philosophy of awakening of the 'Kuṇḍalinī'.

However, dance communicates much more including valuable information on social conditions conditioning evolution of dance form, items that convey the changing hues of socio-political situation, movements and gestures that mirror village life, glimpse of the evolution of language, dressing habits including information on the practice of wearing nose pin and the veil as well as environment.

Attitudes have determined and shaped dance forms. Disapproval and approval have seen giving dance frontiers new extensions and dimensions. When taken only as temple worship, its repertoire was limited and had a particular direction and approach. When it became socially accepted in normal life with its practice being encouraged by educated and enlightened families, its appearance on formal stage proscenium gave it another hue. Entry of educated, articulate members of society in the world of dance further gave it new expressional dimensions. In the history of Kathak, it is said that two Kathaks, Narayan Bhatt and Ghamand Deva from Alwar, laid the foundations of the Raas Leela of Vrindavan that has now become a distinct part of our tradition.

Tenth century onwards there was a visible shift away from Sanskrit in favour of regional languages and dialects. From early twentieth century, Hindi made its inroads, as was being done by English texts, almost at the end of the twentieth century in few special productions. Regarding the textual content or theme of dance, Rādhā seems to have become a favourite subject for delineation only from the 12th or 13th century. Major Gods, even though forming central pillars of the classical fraternity, did not preclude inclusion of local deities. Texts were influenced by prevailing social ethos, which found its way into dance. That trend continues till today.

'Solah Shringar' (or beautification) of the maidens has been an eternal subject for poets, sculptors and dancers. Kālidāsa's description of the heroine in his *Kumārasambhava* written around AD 400 focusses on an uninhibited description of the full youth of the maiden:

> wearing an apparel of the colour of the rising sun and bent forward with her heavy breasts, her movements were like that of a creeper heavy with buds.[1]

In fact 'ghunghat' seemed to be absent from the texts of those periods.[2] It may be presumed that it was not much in vogue and hence did not form an important part in dance delineations. It was shortly, after the Bhakti-Kal (period of religious renaissance) that there are references to the 'ghunghat' (veil). Romance was suggestive and was personified by shy glances of the eyes ('nazar'), quivering lips and trembling hands and long tresses of hair in contrast to the earlier explicit references to romantic fervour. Thus, 'ghunghat ki gat' (gait showing the drawing of a veil across the face) and various kinds of glances through the diaphenous veil became part of the kathak repertoire.

ghunghat ke pat khol ri tohe piya milenge (Kābir)

(i.e. "draw the veil away from your face for your beloved is standing before you". Here, the beloved refers to God).

OR

kabahun mile naina gori se, ghunghat kadhe aur khari se

During any shringar episode, donning of bangles or 'kangāna' is a common movement as is the breaking of bangles to denote a tragic circumstance. However the association of glass bangles with marriage and widowhood came into vogue in medieval India. While green and red glass bangles became a symbol of 'saubhagya' or married woman, breaking of glass bangles became synonymous with widowhood. Reference to glass bangles appear in Sanskrit literature only from the 11th century onwards. One of the earliest references to glass bangles is found in Somesvara's *Suratotsava*.

Similarly, early texts do not seem to have reference to nose pins or nose rings but medieval literature does. And therefore it is no coincidence that yet again in the context of shringar, movement of wearing or denoting a nose ring or a nose pin is as common as their textual visibility.

Change of venue and change of the time of the performance too, influenced development of dance movements where use of lights was concerned. I quote excerpts from one of my articles.

A voyage into the annals of our classical dances takes us ab initio to ritualistic dancing that were performed in an atmosphere permeating with incense and small oil lamps. It is worth noting that the expressions and the tenor of dance movements when performing a prayer are quite different from that when used as a bridge between the congregation and the self. The first necessarily throws accent on sublimation involving minimalist movements and expressions for meditation and requiring minimal lights so as to enable a journey inwards! How can 'pratyahāra' (shutting out outward impressions), 'dhāraṇa' (concentration) and 'Dhyāna' (meditation) be achieved when full lights seem to play a tantalizing, demonic game luring the impressionable outward mind? On the contrary, more lights are required when it comes to story-telling and explaining as actions and expressions become more pronounced. The flickering flames of a series of oil lamps served to cast mysterious shadows around. The movements were contained responding to the needs of the illuminated areas, highlighting the use of 'upāngas' (minor limbs). Every delicate nuance could be seen and appreciated, be it the flick of a wrist, the raising of a brow, the rolling of the eyes, the flutter of the fingers! Thus, the delineation of 'thumrī bhāva' in Kathak could reach a high point in its myriad expressions, creating an aura of romanticism, glamour that could be so inviting and oh' so alluring! Subtlety and finesse became the key words.

Historically, from the candlelight and oil wick lamp era, next came the turn of the gas lamp era. In this era, the tenor of evening and night performances underwent a slight change. The extent of the performing area that could be covered by the illumination from gas lamps extended manifolds. In a way, the performer stood between an illusionary meeting of a night and day performance. Then imagine the reaction of a performer and the audience when the era of electric lights came in. Lo and behold! Daylight at night! Flooded with lights, an illusion of infinite space could be created! What freedom! No more need for extremely contained movements because by now the performers of various styles had got used to spatial movements. The performer could let himself go in the barrage of movements involving various bhangīs, chārīs, bhramarīs, leaps and jumps. Outward display of expression could afford to become more dramatic.

But there was an innate hunger for change that was present within each member of the audience as well as the performer. Each desired to live in a world of illusion, even though momentarily and to be able to seek mystery. Such an unspoken wish coupled with further technical developments has surfaced

> hesitatingly and slowly, engulfing us all. Three-dimensional approach to lighting was adopted where necessary, for thrust areas. Once again, the mystic romanticism of the limited space of illuminated area of the candlelight era, is sought to be re-created – but with one difference. The usage of space and its impact on movements are now being extremely intelligently enhanced by the use of lights. The artiste is once again being able to share the beauty of expansive and contained movements as well as the use of minor limbs.

Purpose associated with this form of communication also had its impact. Purpose of dance as an expression of personal experience differed vastly from its exposition as a medium of communication. Migration of artistes too led to subtle changes and influences – so subtle that far reaching changes that had been incorporated became visible only in hindsight. It is quite common to argue that mythological episodes and legends are irrelevant today and that classical dance is in a time warp. Perhaps a deeper analysis reveals its relevance in no uncertain terms and in a far more effective manner. In case we open the windows of our mind and see that the legend relating to Gaṇeśa's elephant head is actually telling us about the limits of anger, subjugation of Kāliya serpent by Lord Kṛishṇa is asking us to recognize the necessity of all beings to strive for ecological balance, and the episode of disrobing of Draupadī not only as unbecoming problems of society that are still visible today but also if extended in environmental terms as the rape of environment, the legitimacy and relevance of such episodes performed by dancers become extremely meaningful.

Then there is the question of changing aesthetics in every age, for every age has defined beauty differently and these have been communicated through detailed execution of curvature represented in sculptures that with time gave way to more simplicity and directness of expression. The changes with time in the execution of Kathak, for example, speak volumes; for example, in the traditional rendering of solo kathak, extensive use of wrists, 'mukhābhinaya' (facial) and 'upāṅga' (minor limbs) of the dances of the last centuries was a necessary part of rhythmic dexterity. Even around the middle of the twentieth century, effort was made to dance out through the 'angas' (hands, wrists, body and feet) every 'bol' (rhythmic mnemonics) of the pattern. The trend in the sixties of this century was lessening of the arm movements while executing patterns at fast tempo, maintaining however, the full extension and bend of the body from the waist wherever required. The eighties and the nineties saw further reduction in the extension of the arms while dancing at fast tempos. Similarly, the position of the elbows that assumed a higher position in the basic yogic position was lowered over the years. As a result of these changes and changes in attitudes thereof, movements of the present generation of dancers vary greatly from the dancers of earlier generations even within the same gharana.

But these are about changing ages. However the artiste too changes for with passing years, he adds maturity, experience and confidence. Thought processes of artistes keep undergoing sea changes that get reflected in their works. A comparison of elements of dance taught by the same guru to different batches of students over a span of several decades does strengthen this point.

Frontier of dance extends to the realms of 'āhārya' and 'vādya' too. It is commonly felt that the 'churidar-angarkha' were imported in to our country in the last 400 years. However statues of Maurya and Gupta periods do reveal the existence of this form of dance attire namely the 'churidar-angarkha'[3] along side the long skirts or 'lehengas'. Al-Beruni's comments about the dressing habits of Hindu India clearly mention the dhotī, the 'kurtakas' (kurtas), the lehenga and the salwars. It may therefore be deduced that the practice of donning the angarkha-churidar or the kurta-pyjama costume perhaps took a back seat for a few centuries and re-emerged with a new vigour and expression during the Mughal period.

The paths to realization of beauty and aesthetic experience can be many. Means adopted could range from the loudest of expression to the subtlest. Every dance form therefore, has its own hallmark and yet within a dance form, shades vary and within the given overall parameter, one can find ranges of dramatic or the subtle.

What is the scenario today and what are the concerns? It seems to have become common for choreographers and performers to extend the traditional vocabulary with modern-dance techniques, such as curving and tilting the body away from the vertical line, working on or close to the floor, and using turned-in leg positions and flexed feet; of mixing various elements of martial art forms as they provide the requisite ingredients just described. Why does it happen? Is it a recent phenomenon? There is much talk about limitations of a classical style and therefore, the urgent need to extend its frontiers to incorporate and include elements from environment or other styles that would bolster or enhance and successfully depict the message or emotion. However, the real issue is the honesty of the impulse from within. If an artiste believes that by stretching out, he or she is able to express successfully, then so be it. Yet, simultaneously, there are many artistes who are so deeply immersed in the spirit of their own classical tradition, that the question of limitations of their dance form poses no issue at all. They have been able to express, emote and convey successfully whatever they have wanted to convey within their tradition.

In Western context, modern dance developed in the early 20th century as a series of reactions against what detractors saw as the limited, artificial style of movement of ballet and its frivolous subject matter. Perhaps, it may be the same impulses applying in our sub-continent for there have been many efforts in this direction, with Uday Shankar being a pioneer.

The concerns today are many. Do such incorporations or expressions dilute the dance scene or they creating newer forms of dance expression? Do they tamper or dilute the essentials of a dance form? Are some of the changes or incorporations necessary or justified? Does extension towards newer horizons affect classicality and tradition? These are furthered by other introspective questions such as what is meant by 'classicality' and 'tradition'.

The answer, to my mind, is that no one lives in a vacuum. There cannot be any growth in a vacuum and if there is a dynamic environment around, we are all part of this dynamic process called change. But motivations for an artiste comes from within, for each artiste is born with his own individual approach, manner of thinking and therefore, will mould the plastercine in his hands accordingly.

Then what becomes of traditions, may be asked. But a counter question is as to what is meant by tradition itself. A 'tarānā' or a certain rāga or a 'thumri' *per se*, may form part of a tradition today, but they themselves were fruits of newer frontiers of yester ages – as would many other components of our art forms! How many? Difficult to say or even hazard a guess! But what is a fact that many of these traditions have passed the 'test of time' and are with us today.

Similarly, what constitutes 'classicality'? Let us see the ever-expanding range of the Indian classical dance scenario. Just over 50 years ago, there were only four recognized classical dance forms. The number increased to seven about a decade and a half later. As of now, we have eight as Sattriya has joined the ranks of classical dances since the year 2000. Even in the realm of modern dance, what Martha Graham and Isadora Duncan stood for and practiced, are slowly taking on the hue of 'classical' for in this present day world, expressions such as 'classical modern dance' have begun to surface.

Thus changes have been taking place, are taking place and will always be taking place. Overall aesthetics is important and has to be kept in mind! Ultimately it is the 'real breathing' and 'living of every moment'.

NOTES AND REFERENCES

1. canto III.54 आवर्जिता किञ्चिदिव स्तनाभ्यां वासो वसाना।
   पर्याप्तपुष्पस्तबका वनभ्रा संचारिणी पल्लविनी लतेव।
2. *Nāṭyaśāstra*, vol.3, chap. xxiv, p.224
   अवगुण्ठनसंवीता गच्छेत्तु कुलजाङ्गना
   Bharata maintains that an upper caste lady should be seen as appearing in veil. Obviously Kālidāsa knew Bharata's this recommendation; *Abhijñāna Śākuntala*, act V, after verse 18.
   गौतमी - जाते, मुहूर्त मा लज्जस्व अपनेष्यामि तावत्तेऽवगुण्ठनम्। ततस्त्वां भर्ताभिज्ञास्यति।
   Here *avaguṇṭhana* stands for veil (R.V.).
3. Kanishka's headless standing statue kept in the Mathura Museum shows him dressed up in tight fitting long coat and tight fitting pant. Depiction of Kanishka's pant may be taken as the prototype of the laterday churidar pyjama, no doubt a foreign influence coming from Central Asia. But, it remained confined only to royalty (R.V.).

Appendix I
Facts File

1. The Solar System came into existence some 4,600 million years Before Present (BP) as a spinning cloud of gas and dust which condensed to create the Sun. And the left over material nearest the Sun formed into the planets – Mercury, Venus, Earth and Mars.
2. Scientists assert that the Earth too had come up at the same time (i.e. 4,600 years BP). However, it was neither fixed on its axis nor it had elements necessary for beginning and continuation of life for the next 2,250 million years BP
3. Primates came into existence in the Pleistocene Age beginning in 2 million years BP (*Oxford Dictionary*). According to more convincing reckoning, Primates – the Great Apes – emerged as aboreal or denizens of trees some 7 million years BP.
4. Hominid predecessor of the Modern Man was also a member of the Primate sub-category and he too lived on the trees for the first 2 million years of his early existence. Suddenly, he descended on the Earth some 5 million years BP.
5. This new Hominid tried to stand up on his legs and to walk on his feet. His bi-pedalism contributed to several morphological changes in his body. Thus, he became homo erectus.
6. His eating habits (comprising of roots and fruits) were dominated by mental horizons of Primates. This continued till 2.5 million years BP when he continued to remain herbivore. His cranial capacity did not exceed 800 cc which happened to be 100 cc less than that of Chimpanzee. At

the end of that period, sudden climatic changes brought him on the verge of starvation leading to his survival instinct come into play. He suddenly became omnivore (herbivore and carnivore alike).

7. Hominid cranial capacity had originally made him an inferior member of the Primate family. But his 2.5 million years BP eating habits leading to inclusion of a rich quantity of proteins improved his cranial capacity. He became superior to his Primate cousins by crossing their 900 cc cranial capacity limit.
8. The Neanderthal predecessor of the modern man had much greater cranial capacity (ranging between 1200-2000 cc.), but he had to fight against extremely severe cold conditions. He had to work out survival strategies which left him with no amount of surplus energy or capacity to indulge into areas of mental exercise like invention of language.
9. With much smaller cranial capacity (that is, 900-1600 cc.) the homo-sapiens sapiens or the modern Intelligent Man was successful in inventing language some 1 million years BP. He perfected it (language) during the course of the next 9 lac and odd years.
10. It may appear strange that he needed so much time for seeing, hearing, registering in mind, copying and borrowing from nature and animal world the three levels (high, medium and low) of different sounds, tones, tunes and rhythms, as well as adjusting them into word relation sound, and ascribing them definite meanings. This word relation meaning context helped him in creation of meaningfully relevant sentence structures.
11. Latest by 18,000 years BP, homo sapiens sapiens of the Upper Palaeolithic Age had evolved their social, economic, religious and magical traditions. And had also developed high level of their artistic qualities seen in their Rock Shelter Paintings existing across different continents, but sharing the same cultural milieu and traditions. Their paintings not only have pictorial excellence but also have story telling capacity of illustrated paintings of later periods (like the life of the Buddha depicted in the stone sculpture reliefs of Sanchi and Bharhut the quality of documentary films). And,

12. Birth and introduction of writing system in the third millennium BC by the civilizations of the ancient world happens to be the visual counterpart of the oral communication system known for its much, much, greater antiquity and tradition.

(R.V.)

Appendix II
Pioneer of Television

BAIRD WAS DESCRIBED AS A SELF-TAUGHT INNOVATOR

John Baird was born on August 13, 1888, in Helensburg, Scotland.

He went to school at Larchfield, received a diploma in electrical engineering at the Royal Technical College and studied for his B.Sc degree at the University of Glasgow. His studies were interrupted by the outbreak of World War I.

Baird entered in 1914 the military service in a temporary post as electrical engineer. Persistent ill health caused him to resign this post that he held during the war years.

He had to abandon three successive business ventures in Glasgow, the West Indies and London.

In these unpromising circumstances, he turned to amateur investigations, first at making artificial diamonds in which he failed.

In 1922, he retired after a complete breakdown to live at Hastings. He was aware that different forms of electromagnetic radiation, of which visible light was only one, might be used to illuminate a person or object being televised.

He soon discovered that infrared radiation was almost as effective as light.

Baird developed a system for transmitting pictures by the use of infrared rays. He called it 'Noctovision' and the received 'Noctovisor', since it was a night seeing eye.

He explored also the use of very short radio waves to illuminate an object. He published a paper "An account of some experiments in television" in The Wireless World and Radio Review, May

1924. on October 30, 1925, Baird was successful in transmitting his first picture, the head of a dummy. He was keen to obtain publicity and visited the office of the Daily Express newspaper.

The news editor was terrified, as one of his staff reported, "For God's sake, go down to reception and get rid of a lunatic who is down there. He says he has got a machine for seeing by wireless!"

After two years' research, he contrived a primitive apparatus: his electro mechanical system consisted of a light sensitive camera behind a rotating disc.

It delivered a crude picture consisting of 30 lines at twelve frames per second to a television receiver that displayed an uneven and tiny orange and black image.

In 1927 Baird demonstrated television by telephone line between London and Glasgow. He formed the Baird Television Development Company, which on 30 September 1929 was allowed to provide the first BBC television programme.

Synchronization of sound and vision was achieved a few months later, and half-hour programmes were shown regularly of five morning week. These acquired considerable publicity, when they screened the 1931 Derby.

The first formal report of the ability of television signal to provide the range of signals reflected from an object was published by Professor Edward Appleton in Wireless World, January 1931.

Though his main research was devoted to the study of ionosphere, he was a part-time consultant to Baird Television Co. he advised the company on employing cathode-ray tubes and ultra-short waves. So the Baird Company started experimental ultra-short wave television transmissions in April 1932.

In January 1935, the 30-line pictures of primitive television were discontinued. For two years, Baird's company operated side by side with its rival, which had the resources of the Marconi organization behind it.

Baird's system, working on 240 lines, mechanically scanned, and then finally gave place to the 405-line electronically scanned system promoted by Marconi-EMI.

Baird was described as a self taught innovator who matched inventive wits against the pooled ability and the resources of great laboratory physicists.

He was at the forefront of virtually all developments in television and continued research into colour, stereoscopic and big screen television until his death (June 14, 1946)

(Biographical Dictionary of Scientists, Harper Collins, 1994)

R. Parthasarathy, "Pioneer of Television – Baird – a self – taught Innovator"

Biographical Dictionary of Scientists, 1994, The Hindu, 23/2/2006.

Appendix III
Beyond Books...

NOT ALL PEOPLE REALIZE THAT 'COMMUNICATION IS THE MOTHER OF EXISTENCE'

Communication forms the basis for business, relationships and all nuances in the world. Lack of communication leads to ineffectiveness and hampers personal life to a great extent. It is rightly said that 'necessity is the mother of invention,' but not all people realize that 'communication is the mother of existence.

Though India boasts of having the IT offshore capital, with a million engineers in the subcontinent, it is the same set of organizations in the industry, which build state of the art facilities and infrastructure for training their employees. Training in these places starts with the basics of teaching the new recruits communication and soft skills.

This process sounds a bit odd to me because the number of days a new recruit sits in the training is equal to the number of unproductive days from that employee for the organization. Training on the functional skills is mandatory for the employee to turn productive, but training on attitudinal skills is something which, I feel, is happening very late for the individual in his life. This is exactly the gap one of the largest employers in the Indian economy, the IT industry, faces and they are forced to follow this process.

The problem starts with the educational system prevailing in the country. Books, books and books is what the system preaches. Every child after a strenuous schooling is left out to the real world to face the harsh reality blindfolded and that is where the actual learning begins.

Our system has not failed in filling the grey cells of the students to the best, but what is needed is refining their personality by a blend of soft skills to help them realize their potential.

The importance of communication is something which has to be taught young when in uniforms, and not at a later stage in a centralized air conditioned class room by a personality development trainer. Being taught communication and problem solving skills at a later age makes them view these as tools to enhance their success propositions in their work life, little realizing that it should be part of one's character to communicate effectively and come with a problem solving mindset rather than providing quick fixes.

Now what could be done? The deciders of a future economy are the students of the present economy, but some one called a teacher (I would rather call them mentors and sculptors of the future economy) is required to catalyse the mindset of the future economy. A mediocre teacher teaches, a good teacher motivates, an excellent teacher inspires. I urge the teaching society not merely to teach but to mentor.

There is something beyond books and grades. The system has to get out of red tape and mediocrity. Every school should teach students to remove such words as mediocrity and compromise from their dictionary. Teach them about the power of dreams, passion, having a subject like biography or autobiography and tell those stories from the Wings of Fire, Made in Japan and many more. Every student should know about the great dreamers and achievers such as the Akio Moritas, the Ambanis and the Einsteins.

A very pragmatic and radical approach towards education is bound to take this nation to greater heights and would make the future citizens of the country to question the answers rather than answering the questions.

An educational system should foster a culture of change, a culture of dreaming high with a personal vision and a culture which would breed confidence in children. It is the sole responsibility of the educational system to blend the personality of the students at a young age and not that of the industry to start from scratch.

The Hindu, 18/12/2005

Bibliography

SANSKRIT WORKS

Atharvaveda.
Bhagavadgītā.
Bharata, *Nāṭyaśāstra*, (ed.) N.P. Unni, Delhi, 1998.
Kālidāsa, *Abhijñāna Śākuntala*
——, *Kumārasambhava.*
——, *Mālavikāgnimitra.*
——, *Raghuvaṁśa.*
Mahābhārata (Critical Edition)
Pāṇini, *Ashṭāddhyayī.*
Rao, P.S.R. Appa (ed.), *Abhinaya Darpanam.*
Ṛigveda.
Sāmveda.
Vālmīki, *Rāmāyaṇa.*
Varahamihira, *Brihajjataka.*
Vishṇu Purāṇa.
Yajurveda.

GENERAL BIBLIOGRAPHY

Arora, A.C., *Bharatiya Itihas ka Mughal tatha British Kal* (Hindi), Jalandhar, 1985.

Basham, A.L. (ed.), *A Cultural History of India*, Oxford, 1975, Delhi, 1984.

Brook, Peter, *The Shifting Point*, Random House.

Chakravarty, K.K. and R.G. Bednarik, *Indian Rock Art in Global Context*, Bhopal, 2004.

Childe, V. Gordon, 'The Urban Revolution', *The Town Planning Journal*, XXI, Liverpoole, 1950.

Clarke, Arthur C., *Extra Relays: Wireless World*, October, 1945.

Colino, Stacey, *That Look, It is Catching*, The Washington Post.

Dani, A.H., *Indian Palaeography*, Delhi, 1986.

Danial Lerner, Wilbur Sehramm, *Communication and Change in the Developing Countries*, 1967.

Diringer, David, *Writing*, London, 1962.

Flood, Gavin, *An Introduction to Hinduism*, Cambridge, 1996.

Gai, G.S., *Introduction to Indian Epigraphy*, Mysore, 1986.

Gelb, I.J., *A Study of Writing*, 1969.

Ghosh, A., *The City in Early Historical India*, Simla, 1973.

Glatston, *Internet*, 1979.

Gopichand, T., *Otorhinolaryngology*, 1994.

Gupta, S.P., *Elements of Indian Art* (second edn.), New Delhi, 2006.

Hartman, Paul, B.R. Patil and Anita Dighe, *Media and Village Life*, (1992).

Joshi, P.C., *Communication and National Development*, 2002.

Khushu, O.P., *Satellite Communication in Asia: An Overview*, Media Asia, Vol. XX No.1.,1993.

Majumdar, R.C. and K.K. Dasgupta (eds.), *A Comprehensive History of India*, Vol. III, Delhi, 1981.

Majumdar, R.C. and A.D. Pusalkar (eds.), *The History & Culture of the Indian People*, Vol. II; *The Age of Imperial Unity*, Vol. III, Bombay, 1990; *The Classical Age*, Bombay, Vol. IV, 1953, 1962; *The Age of Imperial Kanauj*, Vol. V, Bombay, 1993.

Majumdar, R.C., A.D. Pusalkar and A.K. Majumdar, *The Struggle for the Empire* (eds.), Bombay, 1989.

Maqbool, Mohammad, *Text Book of Ear, Nose & Throat Diseases*, 1982.

Misra, Sunil, *Overview of Communication Research in India*, (1989).

——, *Voluntary Action in Health and Population: Dynamics of Social Transition*, 2002.

Palchun, V.T. and N.L. Voznesensky, *Diseases of the Ear, Throat & Nose*, Mir Publishers, Moscow, 1998.

Pandey, A.B., *Early Medieval India*, Allahabad, 1960, 1993.

Pathak, K.B., 'Kālidāsa and the Hūṇas of the Oxus Valley', *Indian Antiquary*, Vol. XLI, 1914.

Rajan, Mohan Sundara, *The Telecom Story*, Delhi, 1996.

Raychaudhuri, H.C., *Political History of Ancient India*, Calcutta, 1953.

Sarnath Museum Catalogue.

Schevill, Ferdinand, *A History of Europe*, London, 1947.

Shanmugham, A.V., *Communication Research in India*, 1983.

Sharma, G.D., *Reaching Out to All with Quality Higher Education: The Philosophy, Approach and Methodology Towards the Use of EDUSAT Network in Higher Education*, CEC Television News, December 2005.

Sharma, R.S., *Perspectives in Social and Economic History of Ancient India*, Calcutta, 1953.

——, *Urban Decay in India*, Delhi, 1987.

Sinha, Arvind and K.M. Parmar, *INSAT Affects Study Television and Rural Life*: A Closer Look, Technical Report ISRO, January, 1995.
Sircar, D.C., *Numismatic and Epigraphical Studies*, Calcutta, 1973.
——, *Select Inscriptions*, Vol. I, Calcutta, 1942, 1965.
Srivastava, A.L., *Medieval Indian Culture*, Agra, 1975.
Stanley, Baran and Davis Dennis, *Mass Communication Theory*, 2002.
Vajpeyi, Raghavendra, 'Gupta Perception of Indian Reality and Feudalism', in *Proceeding of the Indian History Congress*, 1987.
Vatsyayan, Kapila, *Mudras: The Language of Hands*.
Verma, T.P., *The Palaeography of Brāhmī Script*, Varanasi, 1971.
Washburn, S.L. and C. Jay Phyllis (eds.), *Perspectives on Human Evolution*, USA, 1968.